DOUBLE TROUBLE AT THE PIONEER TUNNEL

TOMMI POCKETS BOOK THREE

MARSHA HUBLER

COPYRIGHT NOTICE

Double Trouble at the Pioneer Tunnel

First edition. Copyright © 2021 by Marsha Hubler. The information contained in this book is the intellectual property of Marsha Hubler and is governed by United States and International copyright laws. All rights reserved. No part of this publication, either text or image, may be used for any purpose other than personal use. Therefore, reproduction, modification, storage in a retrieval system, or retransmission, in any form or by any means, electronic, mechanical, or otherwise, for reasons other than personal use, except for brief quotations for reviews or articles and promotions, is strictly prohibited without prior written permission by the publisher.

This is a work of fiction. Names, characters, businesses, places, events, locales, and incidents are either the products of the author's imagination or used in a fictitious manner. Any resemblance to actual persons, living or dead, or actual events is purely coincidental.

King James version of the Holy Bible—in the public domain

Cover and Interior Design: Derinda Babcock

Editor(s): Cristel Phelps, Deb Haggerty

PUBLISHED BY: Elk Lake Publishing, Inc., 35 Dogwood Drive, Plymouth, MA 02360, 2021

Library Cataloging Data

Names: Hubler, Marsha (Marsha Hubler)

Double Trouble at the Pioneer Tunnel / Marsha Hubler

160 p. 23cm × 15cm (9in × 6 in.)

ISBN-13: 978-1-64949-361-3 (paperback) | 978-1-64949-362-0 (trade paperback) | 978-1-64949-363-7 (e-book)

Key Words: billiards and pool, small town, friendships, middle-grade & young adult, Salvation Army, values & virtues, mystery

Library of Congress Control Number: 2021945340 Fiction

DEDICATION

Dedicated to the kids of the first "real" Tommi Pockets
Friday Night Fun Club

CHAPTER ONE

ASHLAND, PENNSYLVANIA 1959

"Eight in the corner pocket!" I aim at the cue ball and whack! It smacks the black ball dead center into the pocket, and I win the game. I blow the tip of my cue stick like it's red hot and give Runner my best smile.

"Nice shot," Runner says, his dark, wavy bangs shadowing his gorgeous, chocolate brown eyes. My heart skips a beat as he smiles back and gives me that wink he knows makes me crazy.

We're shooting pool at Post 71, the Salvation Army's hangout in a downtown empty storeroom sandwiched between the Ashland Fire Hose Company and Woolworth's general store. Captain Arlene Masters and Sergeant Bill Shuey run the post. They're busy in the kitchenette in the back right corner of the game room getting pizza, soda, and chips ready for all of us.

It's the third Friday in a different kind of January for Central Pennsylvania, not too cold nor snowy, and as every Friday, it's Fun Night from seven to nine for "Captain Ar's kids."

Besides me and Runner, there are about ten others here, some new kids and some who've been in counseling here as long as me—Reuben, Coochie, Leona, and Trudy. None of them knew me from a rock about a year ago, but now they're my best friends. Some of the kids are playing ping-pong or darts while the others play table games or just crash and gossip.

DOUBLE TROUBLE AT THE PIONEER TUNNEL

Two of the new kids are mini gangsters. Twelve-year-old twins, Gail and Dale Pawson, hail from The Heights, the dumpy part of Ashland, and are these two ever a piece of work. All Dale does is make mad faces at everyone and say, "Aw rats" to practically everything anyone says to him, and Gail's hobby is telling everyone a zillion times that she's "twelve-and-a-half- years old." For their age, they're skinny as a zipper and knee-high to a grasshopper, but their destructive behavior makes up for that. I have to dig down real deep in my heart to find the least bit of patience when I'm around them.

"Okay, Reuben and Leona," I say as me and Runner unscrew our cue sticks and pack them into our carrying cases. "The table's yours."

Reuben leaves the dart game he and Coochie just finished, and Leona grabs a cue stick from the wall rack and heads to the table.

"Hey!" Dale Pawson jumps away from his card table, almost upsets the checker game he was playing with another kid, and charges toward us like a runaway train. "It's me and Gail's turn to play pool!" His face, splattered with freckles like buckshot, is fiery red with anger. He runs to the wall rack and grabs a cue stick. Dressed in a worn-out, pale green T-shirt, raggedy blue jeans, and holey white sneakers, he's only about as tall as the stick and almost as thin.

Gail leaves her jigsaw puzzle at another card table and charges toward us. "Yeah! It's our turn. You said we could shoot after you guys!" Her face, a carbon copy of Dale's, freckles and all, is flaming mad too. The only difference between the twins is their hair. Dale's shaggy dark hair sticks up all over like an obnoxious weed, and Gail's hair is in messy pigtails that look like they were braided about four years ago. She helps herself to a cue stick as she and Dale stare at me, Runner, Reuben, and Leona like we're all poisonous snakes.

"Aw rats, it's our turn!" Dale yells at the top of his lungs, and the room grows dead silent. Every stare rivets on the flaring temper bomb ready to explode at the pool table. I glance at Captain Ar and Mr. Bill, who have zeroed in on the action. Both in their starched Salvation Army uniforms, they look like they're bracing for war!

"No, Dale," Runner says, his tone sharp. "We told you when we started tonight that you'd be third."

"That's right," Reuben says, towering over Dale. Reuben's a gigantic brute of a guy, a football tackle, and could easily pick up the skinny kid and throw him right through the wall.

Gail gets in Leona's face and scowls. "Who says it's your turn? I never heard anybody say we were third."

Leona, in the eighth grade the same as me, is my very, very best friend. She's a real looker, the cheerleader type, with long dark curls that hang down over one eyebrow. She's real easy-going—until now. With cheeks flushed as red as the three ball, she stares fire at Gail. "Look, squirt, back off. You heard Runner. You're third."

I've never seen Leona this mad before. But I know ever since the twins started coming here, Leona has almost lost it more than once with their nasty talk and selfish antics. This might be the night.

Gail throws her stick on the pool table, sending the racked balls all askew. She gives Leona a hard push, causing her to stagger. "Get lost, stupid. It's our turn!"

Now I feel the hair on the back of my neck prickle. Nobody mistreats Captain Ar's pool table and pushes my best friend. Nobody. I grab the stick off the table and lean it against the wall. "Hey, Pawson, cool it!" I hurry around the pool table and step between the two girls. "Gail, knock it off. You'll get to shoot in a little while."

"I wanna shoot now!" she yells and kicks me in the shin, sending a horrible, sharp pain through my whole leg.

DOUBLE TROUBLE AT THE PIONEER TUNNEL

"Ow!" I lift my leg and rub my shin. "Why ... you brat!"

"You little monster!" Leona yells at Gail and grabs my arm to help me keep my balance.

At the other end of the pool table, Dale is using his stick to stab at the balls, making them hop across the table. A ripped cloth on that table would cost, at least, fifty bucks to replace!

"Dale, stop it," I say, still rubbing my shin.

"Let him alone." Gail shoves me so hard I lose my balance again. I manage to grab the table railing and save myself from crashing to the floor.

"Dale, stop that!" Runner grabs the cue stick from him. "You'll tear the cloth!"

"I wanna shoot pool!" Dale takes a swing at Runner, but Runner with his gang smarts shies away and avoids a black eye. He reaches for Dale, but Reuben steps between them.

"Just cool it, kid." Reuben grabs Dale's arm. "You'll get your chance."

Dale yanks away from Reuben, grabs a ball and throws it into a cluster of balls, scattering them all over the table. "Who needs a stick?" he says.

"Dale, stop that!" Captain Ar yells as she and Mr. Bill are already charging toward the fiasco.

The other kids are all stuck in a stare-with-their-mouths-hanging-open mode.

"Do you want me to grab hold of him?" Reuben asks Captain Ar.

"No, you kids back off. Bill and I will handle this." She points at Dale. "Bill, calm him down. I'll get Gail."

Mr. Bill, his brown eyes and cheeks flaming with controlled anger, grabs Dale by the arm and pulls him away from the table. "Settle down, lad!"

When Captain Ar grabs the girl's arm, Gail tries to pull away.

"Let me go!" Gail yells. "I hate you!"

With my leg throbbing, I steady myself, then me and Leona back away as we watch Captain Ar pull Gail toward her, wrapping her arms around the kid in a tight hold. Gail wiggles, throws out a string of nasty words, and tries to get loose. But no way. Captain Ar's arms are like a vice, and her face is as red as everyone else's. I guess, it's a "red face" night.

"All right, all right!" Captain Ar says. "Everyone, calm down. Gail, you and Dale are third on the list. Everyone seemed to hear that earlier tonight but you and your brother."

Captain Ar, with her blonde hair drawn back in a bun, penetrating blue eyes, and starched navy blue Salvation Army uniform with gold buttons, runs this place like a Marine drill sergeant. Believe me, she's nobody to mess with. I don't think that's really sunk into the twins' feeble brains yet. They've only been in counseling less than a month and, somehow, earned the right to be at Friday Fun Night tonight. I know everyone else here is wondering how in a pig's snout the twins got that privilege so quick. We're all sure wishing they hadn't. I'll tell you, it'll be a month of Fridays before they come back to Fun Night again.

While Gail and Dale demonstrate what their uncontrollable, bratty tempers can do and say, Captain Ar and Mr. Bill drag the pair toward Captain Ar's office.

Runner rushes to open the door while everyone just watches Captain Ar and Mr. Bill, who have no choice but to "escort" the screaming, flailing, kicking twins out of the room and into her office.

"Close the door, Runner!" Captain Ar says.

Runner slams the door shut, and while those twins are still screaming on the other side of the wall, I look around the game room. All the kids have the same expression on their faces that I probably have on mine. We're all thinking the same thing.

Those twins are about to face the wrath of Captain Ar.

DOUBLE TROUBLE AT THE PIONEER TUNNEL

"Pockets! Runner! Come here, please."

At quarter to nine, Captain Ar pokes her head out of her office and asks me and Runner to join her.

About an hour earlier when the Pawsons exploded then eventually calmed down, Mr. Bill came out of the office and took charge of the game room activities while Captain Ar did her counseling thing with the twins. Counseling? Huh. It's a good thing I'm not their counselor. I'd be wringing their stupid necks.

I can only imagine what went on in there. I wouldn't be a bit surprised to hear she had to tie those two brats in their chairs to quiet them down.

Now, me and Runner head to Captain Ar's office, and I expect to see the twins with hate draped all over their faces and their skinny bodies slumped in total rebellion in their chairs.

We walk in and ... surprise!

They're gone.

"Have a seat, you two." Captain Ar sits behind her desk that's weighed down with stacks of files.

"Where are the twins?" I ask as we sit.

"Their father picked them up a half hour ago," she says. "As much as they need to be around good kids, it'll be at least a month until they're allowed back here on a Friday night." She leans forward and folds her hands on an opened file.

I'm pretty sure the file isn't mine. Ever since I got my life straightened out, my counseling stopped with Captain Ar. But I have to admit, I miss my times with her. She's been like a mom to me ... a mom I've never had. A real mom.

"Pockets, how's your leg?" she asks. "It looked like Gail gave you a pretty nasty wallop."

"It's throbbing a lot, but I'll live."

"Well," she says, "when you get home, you put ice on that for a while."

"Yes, ma'am."

"How'd you get those twins calmed down?" Runner asks. "They went bonkers over nothing!"

"Patience, persistence, and prayer," Captain Ar says. "I want you to understand something about them. Those two poor kids are love starved. They only act out to get the attention they don't get at home." She stares deep into my soul. "Pockets, you should know how that feels."

I nod. "Yeah, I do know, but I never acted like they do."

"Oh, really?" Captain Ar says tongue-in-cheek.

I glance at Runner, and he's stifling a laugh.

"Oh, all right," I confess. "I guess I was pretty messed up last year."

She gives me that all-knowing smile. "Just last year? If you're referring to your history of running with a gang, breaking store windows, dressing like a boy to shoot pool at Joe's until midnight, almost flunking in school—"

"And getting arrested for running with the Thorns," Runner adds with a sarcastic tone. "I'd say 'messed up' is a pretty good description of you."

"And, Runner," Captain Ar says, "remember from whence you came and how far God has brought you."

"I know. I know." He slumps down in his chair and crosses his legs. "I was nothing but a dirtbag until I came here."

"But now," she says, "things are different with the both of you, aren't they?"

We both nod.

"Since you've accepted Jesus as your Savior and decided to be a follower of his, you've been growing in your faith quite nicely."

"Thanks," we both say.

"But I have a question for you."

We just stare at her.

DOUBLE TROUBLE AT THE PIONEER TUNNEL

"Tell me how you think you responded to the behavior of the twins this evening." Captain Ar relaxes into her chair, folds her hands on the open file, and waits.

I hate when she does that. She forces me to look deep inside my heart and dig out all the rot. I glance at Runner, and he's staring at the floor. I think we're both feeling the same way. We didn't react like we should have. Not at all.

I look at Captain Ar, and she smiles. "Well?"

"We could have done better," I say.

"Yeah," Runner says.

"How could you have done better?" she asks. "What should you have done before things got out of hand?"

"Well," Runner says, "giving the twins their own way wasn't the thing to do."

"Absolutely not," she says.

"I guess we were trying to be big shots and run the show," I say. "We should have talked real quiet to the twins to try to calm them down. If that hadn't worked, we should have asked you to come right away and take charge. I know you would have put a stop to the bad scene immediately."

"That's right," she says. "Bill and I heard the racket and were watching intently, but before we could get to all of you, the fiasco had already gone way too far. Remember, all the other kids look up to you two and watch every move you make. I'm afraid you blew it. One of the signs of a maturing Christian is self-control during a crisis."

"Yup, we blew it," Runner says, and I nod.

Captain Ar slides forward and points at us. "Now look, I'm not trying to make you feel badly. I'm just giving you a little advice that will help you when other times in your life might get out of hand. Proverbs 15:1 tells us, 'A soft answer turneth away wrath: but grievous words stir up anger.' I think I had both of you memorize that verse when you were in counseling here, didn't I?"

"Yes," we both say.

"Just try to remember that verse when you find yourself in situations like this one tonight."

"Okay," I say.

"We'll try," Runner says.

"Well, enough of this," Captain Ar says. "With that bit of advice, I want to ask both of you to do something for the twins. For me."

Now we both slide forward in our chairs, and we're all ears. Maybe we're going to have another billiard seminar with Captain Ar and Ruth McGinnis at the Hot Shot Poolroom in Honesdale.

She gives us her best smile and says, "I want you to spend a lot of time with Gail and Dale."

I look at Runner whose eyes are bugging out of his head, his mouth stuck in the shock mode.

All I can say is, "You've got to be kidding!"

CHAPTER TWO

"Good night, Pockets," Captain Ar says. "And remember, I love you."

"I love you too." I never get tired of hearing those words from Captain Ar. I never heard them from my own mom.

It's nine-thirty on Friday night. After all the kids left Fun Night, I waited for fifteen minutes for Pop to come for me, but he never showed up. I helped clean up the game room, and now Captain Ar is dropping me off at home.

I notice that Pop's car is not parked in front of our house, so he must be tying one on at Malloney's Bar. Even if he had been shooting pool at Joe's, he would have come for me. But when he's AWOL, it's usually bad news, and it takes him a day or two to get his head screwed on right again.

I walk into the house and find my sweet grandma wrapped in her woolen pink bathrobe and sound asleep on the couch in the living room. Our new TV is blaring her favorite program, "The Thin Man." Even though her favorite movie actor is Peter Lawford, she probably slept through most of the show because she's always so tired. Me and Pop think she went back to work way too soon after her heart attack.

I turn the TV off and pat it like it's a cute puppy. The TV was one of the Christmas gifts from Pop, the gambler that

DOUBLE TROUBLE AT THE PIONEER TUNNEL

he is, after he won a thousand dollars taking chances on a raffle a couple months ago. Although color televisions have been for sale for a few years, we didn't have quite enough money for one, so we got this black and white one. It's given us a lot of pleasure, especially after a hard day's work or the ton of homework I might have.

Pop's favorite show is "Gunsmoke." I love a whole bunch of shows, but my favorites are "Leave It to Beaver" and "Father Knows Best." I wish my father knew best. Anyway, we all like "I Love Lucy."

I tiptoe back to the sofa, ease in next to my grandma, and gently touch her arm. I whisper, "Meemaw, wake up. I'm home."

What would I do without my sweet grandma? Everyone else knows her as Mona Heizenroth. She stepped up to the plate when Mom walked out on me and Pop when I was about four. I think Meemaw is beautiful, even though she's paper thin, and she wears a lot of makeup. Layers of make-up. Her eyelashes look like window shades, and her cheeks are in red rouge overload.

For twenty years, she's worked dog hard at an envelope factory up at the top of town and has kept me and Pop fed. Without her working, and a lot of overtime too, we'd probably be in jail for not paying the bills. And even though we don't have much extra money, she goes to Gracie's Hair Fashions every Thursday to get her hair done ... bleached once every three months too! To tell you the truth, that's the only nice thing she allows herself to do with all the bills she has to pay, and I'm glad she does it.

A few months ago, I got a part-time job at the bowling alley downtown to help pay the bills. I don't want Meemaw to overdo it and have another heart attack. And Pop? Well, Mr. Thomas Leland has never worried too much about the bills, even when they pile sky high. Right now, he's working part-time at Teichmans' Garage down on Third and Arch Street. At least Pop helps a little when he's not blowing it on his booze or gambling schemes.

Meemaw slowly opens her eyes and focuses on me. "Oh, Tommi Jo, I'm glad you're home. What time is it?"

"It's a little after nine-thirty."

"Is your father here?" She yawns and sits up straight.

"No. Captain Ar brought me home."

"I guess we both know where he is."

"I'm afraid so, Meemaw."

"Did you have a good time at the post?"

"Um, kinda." I slump back into the sofa and sigh.

"Why? What happened?"

"Remember I told you the Pawson twins started counseling with Captain Ar?"

"Yes."

"Well, somehow they earned the privilege to be there tonight. But they went bonkers when they thought it was their turn to shoot pool when it wasn't. They started a fight right in front of all the kids and even Captain Ar and Mr. Bill!"

"And the twins started counseling only a few weeks ago?"

"Yep. They played hooky from school one too many times. But that's only part of the trouble they've gotten into. They got caught stealing candy bars, wrenches, and matches from the Woolworth, and they started a fire in an old, junked car in their neighbors' backyard right next to their own house. They could have burned the whole neighborhood down! That was the last straw. They're only twelve years old and already have a police record."

"You have to feel sorry for those two," she says.

"That's what Captain Ar says."

"I know their mother, Hattie, from years back. When she married that good-for-nothing Parnell, she had no idea the trouble she was heading for. He comes from a long line of reliefers and lives off the government. The only work he's ever done is bootlegging coal once in a blue moon, bagging all that left-over coal from abandoned mines all by himself. Your father often mentions seeing him at Malloney's."

"Yeah, I've heard Pop mention Parnell. I didn't know he was their dad."

"About the time the twins were born, Hattie had tried to work at the envelope factory, but she couldn't because the twins needed her at home. She's tried different part-time jobs since then. She just can't hold down a full-time job for some reason. Marnie Fetterolf told me Hattie has some kind of sickness that takes her to bed for weeks on end. You can see why those twins are practically raising themselves."

Meemaw struggles to stand, and I help her up.

"Are you ready for bed, Meemaw?"

She saunters toward the kitchen, and I follow her. "I didn't have my coffee yet, Tommi Jo." She heads for the stove.

"Wait, Meemaw." I hurry past her and grab the tea kettle. "I'll heat the water for you. You just relax."

"Thank you, honey," she says as she melts into her chair at the table.

I put water in the kettle, place it on the stove, and give that General Electric a puppy pat. Thanks to Pop's gambling money, we finally got rid of that hateful old coal stove.

I get Meemaw's favorite, bright green mug ready with a spoonful of instant coffee and set it in front of her on the table.

"Thanks," she says with another yawn.

The kitchen door flies open, and in stumbles Pop. His white hair, parted down the middle, is all messed, his glasses are bent and cockeyed, and his lip is cut and dribbling blood down on his chin. His thin body staggers to the table, and he flops in a chair.

"What happened to you?" Meemaw goes to the sink, wets a paper towel, and hands it to Pop.

He eases it against his mouth.

"Pop, what happened? Did you wreck the car?"

"N-Nah," he slurs. "An argument over President Eisenhower at Malloney's went a little too far ... and he hit me."

"Who hit you, Pop?"

"Parnell Pawson."

CHAPTER THREE

Saturday morning at nine-thirty, I slap a summer baloney and cheese sandwich together, shove it in a small paper bag, put on my Phillies baseball cap, grab my jacket, and head toward the kitchen door. "Bye, Meemaw!"

"Tommi Jo, remember to be back here by twelve-thirty!" Meemaw yells from the living room where's she's watching "Captain Kangaroo." She says she knows it's just a kids' show, but it's better than all the dumb cartoons that are on all morning. I'm glad she can just relax for once on a Saturday and not do all that awful overtime that wears her out.

"I know," I yell back. "I have to be at work by one!"

"Oh, and will you bring in the mail before you leave?"

"Sure!" I run to the mailbox on the front porch, grab a handful of letters, and give them to Meemaw. Glancing at the top of the pile, I see something that demands my undivided attention. "Meemaw, there's a letter for me. From Mom!" I take it from the pile and stuff it in my back jeans pocket. "I'll read it at the park while I wait for the other kids. I'm going to get there before any of them."

"Be careful!" she says as I hurry out the door.

"I will!"

The weather in January is still crazy. There's no snow, and it's warm like April. I grab my bike and take off for the Higher Ups Park where I'm going to meet Runner, Leona,

DOUBLE TROUBLE AT THE PIONEER TUNNEL

and Coochie. We said we'd all meet there at ten just to chill out with each other for a while. Runner works with me at the bowling alley for four hours every Saturday afternoon, so I'll get to see him for a whole six hours and twenty-three minutes today.

It takes me about ten minutes to pedal to the park. It's dead quiet, which really surprises me considering how warm the weather is. I settle in at one of the picnic tables, grab Mom's letter, tear the envelope open, and start reading.

> Dear Tommi Jo,
>
> I'm sorry I haven't written to you since before Christmas. Your Aunt Alma and I have been so busy here in Kansas. Besides working overtime at the candy factory, we decided to paint every room in her house a different pastel color. She says it's high time we do that. She bought the house five years ago, and it was already twenty years old. Whoever lived here before loved yellow, and practically everything in the house, including the toilet, all the sinks, and every wall is an ugly yellow. We both felt like we were living in a giant banana. It's a lot of work, but the whole place is looking much better. Last week I read in the Cosmopolitan magazine that the movie star Doris Day loves yellow, but I'm sure her house would never have a total sweep of such a gawdy color.
>
> Speaking of work, do you remember in my last letter I told you about two guys we met at the factory and that they took us to a fancy dinner party at Christmastime? Louie and Roscoe have been helping us paint, so we're getting done much faster than we had

thought. And guess what else we're going to do with those two guys. We're planning a summer trip with them.

At first, we were going to go to Disneyland in Anaheim, California, but we changed our minds. None of us have ever been to New York City, so when the summer rolls around and we all get our two-week vacations together, we're heading east. I can't wait to see the Empire State Building and Wanamaker's huge store. If we have any time left on our way home, I'm hoping we'll be able to stop by and see you and your grandmother for a day or so.

It was real nice to see you again so soon after I moved in with your Aunt Alma out here in Kansas last year. I hope your grandmother is still recovering from her heart attack. When we visited her, she said she planned to start back to work full-time within a week or two. Is she doing that yet? Tell her not to push herself too hard. Your father needs to get his tail moving faster, get a better job, and help more around the house. I guess some things never change.

I know you're probably wondering if we've gone to church. That seems to be the question you ask me most of the time. We had planned to go the last few Sundays, but life just got in the way. Now that the holidays are over, we're going to try real hard to go. I must say that I've noticed how church has helped you to get your life straightened out. I sure wish your father would start going so he could get his act together.

DOUBLE TROUBLE AT THE PIONEER TUNNEL

Well, kid, behave yourself, and I hope you're still thinking about our invitation to move out here with us. We do have a nice third bedroom here. And there's a school just a few blocks away.

Love, Mom

P.S. Write and tell me what you did with the twenty dollars I gave you for Christmas. You didn't buy a pet alligator, did you? Ha ha.

I read the letter twice, and then the tear bottle in my heart overflows and spills out of my eyes. I miss my mom. I've missed her every single day since she left me and Pop. I bury my head in my arms and bawl like a big baby. I want to be with Mom, but I can't move to Kansas. How can I leave Meemaw and Pop, all my friends, and, most of all, Captain Ar, who told me about Jesus and has loved me through a lot of tough times?

As I bawl away, I hear someone coming. I wipe my eyes on my sleeves and look up.

Leona is walking toward me carrying a paper lunch bag, and Runner and Coochie are a stone's throw behind her, biking in my direction.

I fold the letter, stuff it in my jacket pocket, and wipe my eyes again just as Leona gets to the table.

I remember another time when I was bawling here at the park, and Leona showed up. It was before we became friends at all. I did my best to cover up my tears because I thought a tough kid like me doesn't cry in front of anybody, least of all one of the most popular girls in my class. But Captain Ar told me never to be ashamed to shed tears because it helps clean out my heart. So now I don't care who sees me cry over my mother.

"Hi, Pockets," Leona says.

Our eyes lock. She slides next to me and puts her hand on my shoulder. "What's the matter?"

"Oh, the same old thing. I got a letter from Mom, and as usual, she writes to me like I'm some long-lost friend she knew twenty years ago."

"I'm so sorry, Pockets."

I wipe my eyes again as the boys pull in on their bikes. They focus on me, and their faces melt into deep concern.

"Pockets, are you okay?" Runner asks and sits across from me.

"Yeah." Coochie joins Runner. "What's happening?"

A slight breeze whisks through the park and fluffs Coochie's wavy blond hair off his brown, puppy dog eyes. He's one of the cutest boys in my eighth-grade class at Ashland Junior High. A while back I had a crush on him until I met Runner.

Coochie Montgomery loves to shoot pool and has gotten pretty good. I guess that's why we're good friends now. Although he sometimes gets under everybody's skin with his bossiness, I still like him a lot. A long time ago, I gave up wanting to tell him to shut the hole in his face when he tries to rule the universe. Captain Ar told me she's proud of me for holding back my nasty tongue when Coochie might have deserved a few choice words.

Runner stares at me and gives me a cockeyed smile. "Pockets, your eyes are almost as red as your cap. Hey, I haven't seen you wear that thing in a long time, like since you stopped shooting pool at Joe's. I thought you gave up the cap when you stopped going to the poolroom."

I sniffle and wipe my nose on my sleeve. "I pretty much have, but once in a while I wear it, just because."

"So why all the tears?" Coochie asks. "Did something happen to your grandma again?"

"No, she's doing pretty good." I pull the letter out of my pocket, wave it, and return it to my jacket. "This is a letter from my mom. She never writes to me as a daughter but instead—just like some long-lost friend. She also wants me to go and live with her, which really doesn't make any sense because she's never really had much time for me since I was four."

"You're not going to move, are you?" Leona asks.

Worry is draped all over the group's faces.

"I don't know how I can leave all you guys and Meemaw, Pop, and most of all, Captain Ar. I just can't."

Big, wide smiles wipe away the worry.

"Well, I for one am glad." Runner winks at me. "I don't want to lose my pool shooting buddy."

I feel my cheeks flush red hot then notice the six swings swaying in the gentle breeze on the far side of the ball field.

"As nice as it is today," Runner says, "we should have brought our ball equipment or something like that. This is really nice weather for January."

"Nah," Coochie says. "I'm not in the mood for games. Pockets, what did Captain Ar want with you and Runner in her office last night? Runner's been tight-lipped."

"It's not a secret, is it?" Leona brushes her hair back off her eyebrow in true cheerleader style.

"I don't think so," I say and look at Runner.

"I guess not," he says.

"She wants us to work with the twins to see if we can help *civilize* them," I say with a cautious smile.

"You're kidding," Coochie says. "Work with those two brats? They're hopeless."

"It seems that way," Runner says. "But Captain Ar keeps reminding us how far all the rest of us have come since we had counseling. Some of us were hopeless a while back."

"Yeah," I say. "She always says that tough love and counseling with verses from the Bible will help any kid, no matter how much trouble they've been in."

"Well," Coochie says, "I know for a fact I wouldn't be able to keep my cool if I'd have to try to work with those twins, especially after seeing how they acted last night. They're little monsters. I'd probably smack them, and I'd be back in counseling with Captain Ar quicker than you could smack *me* in the head."

"What are you going to do with them?" Leona asks. "And when?"

"We don't know yet," Runner says. "Captain Ar wants Pockets and me to meet her Monday after school, and she'll tell us what she has in mind."

"Better you than me," Coochie says. "If those two brats won't even listen to Captain Ar and Mr. Bill, I'm sure they're not going to bow to your requests without a knock-down-drag-out fight. This is going to be very interesting."

Runner points toward the swings and whispers, "Hey, look who just came on the bikes over there."

"Why, it's the twins," Leona says.

We all watch as they get off their bikes. In dirty tank tops and ragged jeans, the twins untie something from their bikes and head toward the swings.

"What do they have?" Coochie asks.

"It looks like Dale has a hatchet," I say. "What's he doing with a hatchet?"

"And I think Gail has a baseball bat," Runner says. "Now what are they up to?"

I watch as the two saunter closer to the swings, and my open mouth gets stuck in neutral. *Are they going to do what I think they're going to do?*

It doesn't take long for us to find out.

CHAPTER FOUR

Like an invading army, the twins rush toward the swings and attack them, chopping and pounding the wooden seats. The swings recoil from the blows, bouncing and twisting on their chains. Finally, Gail whacks a swing so hard, it breaks loose from its one chain, dangles, and drags on the ground. Relentless at his victim, Dale hacks its seat, chips of wood flying everywhere.

"We've got to stop them," I say, "or they'll destroy every swing!"

"I don't think they even noticed us," Leona says.

"Let's go," Runner says.

"I'd like to wring their necks," Coochie says. "Just let me at them."

"Now wait," I say. "How would Captain Ar want us to handle this? We can't go charging down after them. They might attack us!"

"Well, we have to do something—and right now," Runner says.

"Let's just meander over to them and ask them to join us for lunch," I say. "We could tell them they won't be able to come to Friday Fun Night for a while if they don't stop."

"But we only have enough food for our own lunch," Coochie says. "I brought only one measly sandwich."

"They can have mine," I say.

"Mine too," Runner adds.

DOUBLE TROUBLE AT THE PIONEER TUNNEL

"Sounds like a plan," Leona says. "Let's try it."

"C'mon," I say.

We cautiously move away from the picnic table and saunter toward the twins.

"Smile, everybody," I whisper.

About halfway across the ballfield, I say to the twins, "Hi, kids. What are you guys doing?"

The twins stop dead in their tracks and stare at us, their weapons raised.

"Hey, you guys," Runner says, "we're having a picnic, and we have some extra sandwiches. Do you wanna to join us?"

Panic blankets their faces like a storm cloud. Dale says something to his sister, then they drop their tools and take off toward the thicket, a tree-covered hill hugging the south side of the park.

"Hey, wait!" Runner yells.

"Come back here!" Coochie yells.

"Where are they going now?" Leona asks.

"I wonder if they know about that old, abandoned coal mine," Runner says.

"An abandoned mine?" Leona says. "Hey, that's right. There is one somewhere in that hill. I remember exploring around back there when I was a kid. I think it's hidden behind all those trees and bushes, and it's not too far from the edge of the park. My dad said the mine closed about fifteen years ago and warned me never, ever to go near it again. Do you think they're heading there? That's so dangerous."

"My dad told me if he ever caught me playing near that, he'd tan my hide," Coochie says. "He also told me the town's officials named it the Pioneer Tunnel and are either going to permanently shut the entrance with dynamite or maybe make the mine into some kind of tourist attraction in a few years."

"Well, I know it's there, but it's all boarded up now," Runner says. "At least, it used to be. The Hawks gang thought of using it as a hideout at one time, but we couldn't get past all the boards across the entrance."

"If they do know about that mine, they could get hurt going inside," I say. "We've got to stop them."

We take off full speed ahead after the twins. I watch them disappear behind a solid border of thick trees and bushes. In seconds, we're making our way through the dense woods with the abandoned mine straight ahead. Its entrance is barely visible, choked out by the wildness of the thick bushes that surround it.

The twins are trying their best to rip off one of the boards sealing the entrance. If they do that, as skinny as they are, they'll easily squeeze through and get into the mine. Without us ripping another board off, we won't be able to go in after them.

"Hey, you kids," I yell as we charge toward them. "Stop that!"

"You better not go in there!" Runner yells. "It's dangerous. You could get killed!"

Our words fall on deaf ears as we catch up to the twins. Runner and Coochie grab Dale, and Runner wraps the screaming, flailing kid in a tight bear hug.

Me and Leona grab Gail, and I wrap my arms around the kid while she kicks and screams.

"Oh, just stop it!" Leona says as she helps me hold down Gail.

"Just quiet down, you two," I try to say calmly. "We're not gonna hurt you."

"Let me go, you scuzz bags!" Dale yells.

"Mind your own fat business, ya creeps!" Gail adds.

"We're not letting you go until you calm down," Runner says. "C'mon. We're going back to the park."

Runner and Coochie lock their arms around Dale's arms, and me and Leona do the same with Gail. We make our way back through the woods with the twins pulling, flailing, and screaming nasty words. Eventually they tire out so we can walk "decent and in order."

"I hate your guts," Gail says. "Leave me go!"

"You finks think you're all hot stuff because you're Captain Ar's pets," Dale fumes.

We stop at the swings and all catch our breaths while still holding on to the twins.

"If the cops would have seen you do all this damage, they would've arrested you," I say.

"Big deal," Dale says.

"And who cares?" Gail says.

"Coochie," I say, "get the hatchet and bat."

He lets go of Dale and picks up both things.

"Now," Runner says, "you kids aren't getting these back."

"They're ours!" Gail says.

"Not anymore," Leona says.

"Are you two gonna behave?" I ask, slowly releasing my grip.

"Yeah, sure," Gail says.

"What's it to you?" Dale says.

"Because we care about you and want to be your friends," I say.

"All right, Dale. Just relax." Runner lets him loose. "You two better head home before the police or groundskeeper sees what you did here."

The twins stare at us, contempt oozing from every inch of their skinny bodies. Without another word, they jump on their bikes and take off like they're being chased by a pack of wild dogs.

But a stone's throw away, Gail slams on her brakes, looks back at us, pauses as if in deep thought, then starts pedaling to catch up with her brother, who's almost out of sight.

This weekend turned out to be just like many others.

When the twins left the park, me and my friends couldn't decide what to do about the broken swings. They sure needed to be fixed, so somebody needed to know. Then we worried if we told on the twins, they'd hate us even more, and we'd never be able to be their friends.

We headed to the basement of the pavilion where birthday parties are held and looked in the window of the office. The door was locked, the room dark, and we couldn't see the park's caretaker anywhere, so we went home. We all agreed to tell our parents and see what they thought we should do.

I was home only a few minutes when the phone rang. Runner told me his dad said he'd call the police station and report it, so we'd have to let the chips fall where they may.

I'm not sure if he was talking about potato chips or the broken swing's wood chips, but they sure fell. I'm hoping it all works out, and the twins won't connect the dots.

Saturday afternoon at five o'clock sharp, me and Runner finished our shift at the Sunset Lanes. Setting the bowling pins with him next to me is no chore at all. Believe me. I brought home four dollars for the eight hours I worked last week. Meemaw says that little bit of cash really helps, especially with the grocery bill. And Pop said the gas price just hit twenty cents a gallon!

Sunday, me and Meemaw went to church, as usual. I love church. Runner and his parents go to the same church, and I get to stare at him all the way through teen class during Sunday school. But I also love to hear Pastor Sutcliff talk about the Bible during the regular service. Sometimes I wonder if Meemaw tells him all about my antics because he often preaches about things that sound a lot like stuff I've done, and then I feel like a big, fat louse.

Captain Ar always tells me those feelings I have are good. It's called "conviction," and all I need to do is ask

God to forgive me. Before I asked Jesus to take control of my life, I didn't care two hoots about any of the rotten things I had done. I thought most of them were really funny. But now, I don't know how running with a gang, breaking windows, sassing Meemaw, smart-mouthing teachers, and flunking school would be funny in anybody's book.

The rest of Sunday I did my homework and watched "The Ed Sullivan Show" with Meemaw in the evening. Pop was probably at Joe's shooting pool.

I miss shooting pool with Pop, but I don't miss Joe's. With all the smoke and gambling and swearing, it's no place for me since I became a Christian. Besides, when all the guys there found out I was a girl in disguise, Joe really didn't want me back anymore. I'm just glad I can shoot at Captain Ar's game room anytime I want, or I'd probably go bananas.

Now it's Monday, and I'm in the school cafeteria with my friends. The seventh, eighth, and ninth graders are eating vegetable soup, baloney sandwiches, and canned peaches for dessert. The weather took a turn toward a real January, so everyone's wearing the sweaters they got for Christmas. Mine is sky blue with a big, fat, jolly snowman in a black top hat plastered all over the front. The weatherman says we might get snow this week. That would be a nice surprise.

Speaking of surprises, Moose, that's Marvin Fenstamacher, joins me, Leona, and Coochie at our lunch table. For the first time ever. He's the typical jock. His light brown hair is in a flat-top, and he's built like a bulldozer. He usually hangs out with "the group," all the other sports nuts and the cheerleaders, but today he's visiting us. He must be up to something.

A couple months ago here in the cafeteria, I had a round with Moose, who thinks the sun rises and sets on him because he made two touchdowns on the JV football team this past season. He called me and Leona losers because we're some of Captain Ar's kids. He made Leona cry. He just made me steaming hot mad. I told him to shut his big mouth and go stick his head in a commode three times and pull it out twice. As usual, I let my temper control *my* big mouth, so a few days later, I built up enough nerve to tell him I was sorry. That was awful hard, but Captain Ar said that saying I'm sorry helps develop my character. I have a lot of character developing to do.

Anyway, now Moose is sitting next to Coochie, and I'm staring at the jock wondering what's up his cocky sleeve. Moose has stopped us all dead in our tracks. We just chew our baloney sandwiches and stare at him.

Coochie finally asks Moose, "So, what's up?"

I look at Moose with a suspicious eye. He's never even said a kind word to me or any of Captain Ar's kids. Now he's got a real funny look on his face. He peeks left then right like he's trying to hide from someone and says almost in a whisper, "I need to ask you all a question."

"What?" I say with a less-than-friendly tone.

"What goes on in your talks with that woman?" he asks.

"What woman?" Leona asks.

"That lady at the Salvation Army," Moose says.

"What's it to ya?" Coochie sneers.

"Look," Moose leans forward and whispers, "I know I've got on your tails before about you going for counseling, and—and I'm sorry. I need to know something about what goes on there at the post. Who's this Captain Masters?"

"Is this some kind of joke?" Coochie asks.

"No," Moose says. "Honest."

"Then why the questions?" I ask.

DOUBLE TROUBLE AT THE PIONEER TUNNEL

Moose looks around again. "If you tell anybody what I'm going to tell you, I'll—"

"Moose, what is it?" Coochie's face flushes red with impatience. Leona is sitting wide-eyed, and I'm just staring holes through the jock.

Moose tightens his lips and whispers, "You probably don't know I have a really bad temper."

"I've seen it," Coochie says. "One time, I saw you punch a hole in the wall in the gym locker room," Coochie says. "Yeah, I've seen your temper in action."

"Well, it got out of hand last Saturday night, and I messed up big-time. My dad and I had a nasty mouth battle, so I took off in his old truck and ran it into a tree. I walked away without a scratch, but the truck is totaled. I got busted, and now I've got to have counseling at the Salvation Army for three months. I just need to know what to expect."

"Are you crazy?" I say. "You're only fourteen years old, and you tried to drive your dad's truck? Did you ever drive it before?"

Moose shakes his head. "I know it was stupid. Now, tell me about that woman. I've heard she's a real tyrant."

I swallow hard to stop myself from laughing right in Moose's face. Here's this super jock, supposedly not afraid of anything, and he's shaking in his boots about Captain Ar.

"Nah," Leona says, "she's nothing like that. Now, she doesn't put up with lying or smart-mouthing, but she really cares about kids. You don't need to worry about her at all."

"If the football team ever hears that I'm going to a counselor, a woman, and at the Salvation Army, I'll be the laughingstock of Ashland High." Moose looks at us with pleading eyes.

Coochie raises his palms toward him. "You don't need to worry about any of us spilling the beans. But as hard as you try to hide it, the news will leak out somehow."

"Listen, Moose," I say. "Just do what she says, and you'll be fine. It's not all torture either. Every Friday night from seven to nine, all Captain Ar's kids can go to the post's game room in the back of the building. It's really a cool place with a pool table, ping-pong table, and lots of other games."

"And there's always good eats too," Leona says. "Like pizza, chips, and soda."

"But you have to earn the right to go to Friday Fun Night," I say.

"How?" A flicker of a smile hints at Moose's lips.

"Just do as Captain Ar says, and you'll be fine," Coochie says.

"Yeah," I say with a smirk. "Maybe in a few weeks you'll be joining the rest of us losers at Post 71."

"Very funny." Moose stands and turns to head back to his clique. "Thanks. See you all later."

And I wonder what kind of tall tale he's going to tell all his buddies.

CHAPTER FIVE

Monday after school, me and Runner report to Captain Ar to get the scoop on the twins and what she wants us to do to try to help them. I'm as excited about this as if I had to swim ten miles in the Arctic Ocean at midnight. We settle in our chairs and get ourselves ready to hear her plan.

The woman gives us her warmest smile all the way to her blue eyes as she opens a file and picks up her pen. "From the look on your faces, may I assume correctly that you're not too excited about working with the twins?"

I release a frustrated sigh and cross my arms. "We already had another run-in with them on Saturday at the Higher Ups Park. They were destroying swings with a hatchet and a baseball bat!"

Runner adds, "When we stopped them, they took off and tried to hide in the Pioneer Tunnel, that abandoned mine in the hill behind the park. But we caught up to them and sent them home."

"We tried to be nice to them at first," I say, "but they just went bonkers like they did here last Friday night. They're just impossible!"

Captain Ar nods. "I know all about them destroying the swings. Because they've been adjudicated into my counseling program, the police called and told me what they did."

DOUBLE TROUBLE AT THE PIONEER TUNNEL

"We can't get to first base with them," I say. "They just hate everybody. Everything."

"Well, we're going to try to change that," she says.

"It'll take a miracle," Runner says.

"I believe in miracles." She smiles again, and her blue eyes penetrate my soul. "I'm looking at two of them right now."

I take a hard gulp and make up my mind to try to never ever disappoint this woman, even if it means trying to help the twins. I glance at Runner, and the look on his face tells me he's thinking the same thing.

"Are you ready to hear what I have in mind?" she asks. "I know it's not going to be easy, but I believe you can reach those two like no one else can."

"Ready," we both say.

"Okay," she says. "I completely understand how busy you two are with school, your work at the bowling alley, and helping out at home. But I'd like you to consider coming here after school every Monday for about an hour or so and then coming at six o'clock on Friday evenings before the other kids come at seven for Fun Night. We've arranged with the twins' parents and the school to have Bill pick up Gail and Dale at dismissal every Monday and bring them here. Bill will also be on standby and pick them up at their home on Friday evening if their dad is 'unavailable.' Unfortunately, Mrs. Pawson has been bedridden the last month or so. She's so sick most of the time, she can hardly do anything with those twins. They're pretty much raising themselves. That whole family needs an awful lot of prayer ... and help."

"But I thought they weren't invited to Fun Night for a while," I say.

"Oh, they're not," she says. "Either their father or Bill will take them home at seven o'clock."

"Oh," Runner says, "that's good. I'd hate to have them attack the pool table again."

"But where will we be with them?" I ask. "Here in your office?"

"No," she says. "You'll be in the game room."

"Huh?" I say. "How will we keep them away from the pool table or any games, for that matter?"

"Hang on, and I'll explain," she says. "Every Monday afternoon and Friday evening, I'd like you to try to befriend them in the game room while you do your homework together. You can all spread out at the card tables. Remember to bring your books, but if you have no homework, then bring some books to read or magazines or something like that. We'll have a snack for you, and no one else will be here for counseling in my office."

I scratch my head and ask, "But what if they head to the pool table?"

"Or the ping-pong table ... or any of the games?" Runner adds.

"Bill and I will have the games all put away and the two tables covered with cloths."

"But what if the twins go bonkers again?" I ask.

"After I get them settled with you, I'll be working in my office with the door opened a crack, and Bill will be *busy* getting your snack ready in the kitchenette. We'll not let anything get out of hand."

"So," I say, "what are we supposed to do?"

"And when do we start?" Runner asks.

"We're going to start this Friday right before Fun Night," she says. "When you all get here, we're going to tell the twins that we've opened up the game room as a study hall for students to get their homework done and get better grades. I believe they're quite intelligent, but because they've neglected their studies for so long, they're failing miserably. I'll also tell them that you two will be glad to help them with their homework if they just ask."

"Fat chance," I say then slap my hand over my mouth. "Oops. Sorry."

DOUBLE TROUBLE AT THE PIONEER TUNNEL

"No, really," she says, "I believe this will work. It might take a while, but as I've told you, those kids are starving for attention. I know they're so incorrigible, no teachers want to spend any extra time with them, and the twins are very close to getting suspended or even expelled if they soon don't get the help they so desperately need. I'm very thankful the judge ordered them here instead of sending them away. With intense counseling and help from kids like you who know how these two feel, I'm hopeful we can help them."

Runner's face is draped in doubt. "So, you really think they'll let us help them? Right now they hate us."

"They don't really hate you," Captain Ar says. "Pushing everyone away is just their defense mechanism to keep anyone from getting close to them. Yet, that's what they crave the most."

"Okay." Runner sighs. "We'll give it a try, but it might take until Christmas."

"Or until we're all old and gray," I say, and we all laugh.

Captain Ar takes the time to write something in her file. Then she looks at us with those piercing blue eyes that make me feel like she's reading my mind. "I'm also going to tell them that if they behave and let you help them with their homework, they'll earn the privilege to learn how to shoot pool. And, my friends, you'll be their instructors."

I raise my eyebrows. "You're kidding."

"For real?" Runner says.

"For real," she says. "That will be one of the motivating factors for them to behave. It might take a while, but if you reach out to them and really care for them, they'll feel that love, something they've never felt before, and I think they'll start to respond in a positive way."

Me and Runner look at each other and trade cautious smiles.

"I'm game," I say.

"Me too," Runner says. "But—"

Captain Ar raises her hand toward Runner. "Let's just be positive about this whole thing. With God all things are possible."

"I know, I know," Runner says, and I nod.

"Now," she says, "before you go, I want to tell you something else that should really excite you both."

"What?" I ask.

"Bill and I have planned to take all our counselees on a two-day weekend snow camping trip next month. The Marching Forward Camp in Wayne County is a Christian facility that has tremendous activities all year round for kids. And here's the best part. The camp is only twelve miles from Honesdale. And you know who's in Honesdale, don't you?" She winks, and I practically jump off my seat.

"Miss McGinnis!" I say.

"And the Hot Shot Pool Room!" Runner slides forward on his chair and almost slips off. "Are we gonna shoot there again?"

"And see Miss McGinnis?" I ask.

Captain Ar relaxes in her chair, folds her arms, and says, "Well, in your language ... yup."

"When are we going?" I ask.

"And who gets to go?" Runner adds.

"We're planning to go the second Friday and Saturday in February. Any of the kids in counseling are invited to go. There's an enrollment fee, which our organization will help pay for those families struggling with their finances. We all need to pray that snow camp *will be* snow camp with cold weather and snow on the ground."

My joy about the whole matter suddenly turns sour like a rotten lemon. "You said anybody in counseling can go?"

"That's right," she says.

"Then you mean the twins can go too?" I ask.

She just nods.

DOUBLE TROUBLE AT THE PIONEER TUNNEL

"They'll ruin everything!" I say.

Runner slumps back into his chair. "And the camp people will probably have all of us leave early and tell us to never come back. Do those twins have to go?"

Captain Ar points her finger at us. "Now wait just a minute. You're forgetting one important thing here. You two need to focus on what I've asked you to do, not on all the fun you were planning to have. You can still have a lot of fun, but I want you to really zero in on befriending Gail and Dale. As far as I know, they've never been away from home for any reason, especially to a camp where they can have a lot of fun. What do you say?"

I nod. "Okay. I'll try my best."

"Me too," Runner adds.

Captain Ar closes the file and stands. "Just remember to pray for God to help you. I know this isn't going to be easy at all, but with his help, I believe you'll both do a great job."

CHAPTER SIX

After me and Runner leave the post, he heads downtown four blocks to his house on Second and Ash Streets. I hightail it seven blocks uptown to Eighteenth and Market and rush into my house, into the kitchen where I know my sweet Meemaw is cooking up a feast. Even though it's Monday, and we usually have leftovers from Sunday's dinner, Meemaw has the day off since she worked overtime on Saturday, so she's working on fried pork chops, baked potatoes, and some of our sweet corn we froze last fall. My mouth waters as soon as I take a whiff of the delicious aromas filling every corner of the room.

"Where's Pop?" I ask. "I thought he only worked until noon today."

"He did," Meemaw says as she flips the pork chops in the frying pan. "But I haven't seen hide nor hair of him all afternoon. He's probably hanging out at Malloney's and wasting his overtime pay. Go ahead and set the table for three anyway. Maybe he'll show up for supper." She glances at the wall clock. "It'll be ready at five o'clock sharp."

"Okay, Meemaw." I proceed to set the table. "I think I can get my homework done before we eat. I only have a few pages of English to finish. And starting next week, I probably won't have any homework to do at home on Mondays or over the weekends. Captain Ar wants Runner

DOUBLE TROUBLE AT THE PIONEER TUNNEL

and me to try to help the Pawson twins after school twice a week with a 'study period' she's setting up just for them. I have no clue how that's gonna work. They don't listen to anyone, especially to kids like us."

"Well, you just try to do whatever Captain Ar wants you to do. I've never met anyone who has such wisdom to deal with kids like she has. I'm sure it'll work out."

"Yes, ma'am," I say. "Oh, and I have to tell you the best news ever. Captain Ar and Mr. Bill are going to take all their counselees—that's what they call us kids—to a snow camp in a few weeks. And it's in Northeast Pennsylvania, close to Honesdale, and we're going to get to shoot pool with Ruth McGinnis again. I'm practically jumping out of my skin just thinking about it."

Meemaw opens the oven door, pokes a baked potato, then shuts the door. "A winter retreat? That sounds wonderful, Tommi Jo. Do you know when you're going and for how long?"

"Captain Ar said—"

"Mona! Pockets! Anybody in there!" Pop's voice echoes from just outside the kitchen door. "Somebody, open the door for me."

I open the door, and Pop charges in carrying two heavy cardboard boxes. "Clear a spot on the table for me," he huffs, struggling to balance his cargo.

I rush to the table and push back one of the place settings.

Pop hurries to the table and plops the boxes down so hard everything on the table does the jig. "Whew! They're heavy!" he puffs.

"What on earth do you have there, Tom?" Meemaw says.

"Yeah, Pop," I add. "What's up?"

"I'm planning ahead, girls," he says. "Planning ahead." He opens one of the boxes and pulls out a bottle of beer.

I examine the box, which has at least a dozen bottles of the same stuff.

"Planning ahead?" Meemaw joins us at the table and throws Pop one of her disgusted scowls.

I know exactly what she's thinking. All of his last week's overtime pay is in these boxes.

"Darn that Parnell Pawson," Pop says. "Every time he shows up at Malloney's, he starts an argument about anything under the sun with anybody stupid enough to play his game. I'm about ready to give him a knuckle sandwich."

"Is that all booze in both boxes, Pop?" I ask. "And why do you have it all here at home?"

"Beer in the one box and wine in the other. I like variety." Pop releases a devilish smile. "And there's no aggravation at home. I can have a drink anytime without the aggravation. I'll give Malloney's a few more tries, but if Pawson is there every time I want to just go in and relax, my days of going there will be over."

I glance at Meemaw, and she just peaks her eyebrows. "Well, Tom," she says, "I guess it'll be nice having you around the house more often. But I have no place here in the kitchen to store all those bottles. Where are you going to put them?"

"I'll keep them in the cellar," he says. "They won't be in your way."

I'm frying my brain through all of this, wondering if this is a good or a bad thing. Pop's never admitted to anyone, especially himself, that he's as close to being an alcoholic as he can get. Maybe him having a beer with his supper will be better than him having three or four at Malloney's after work. But I keep praying he sees how bad it is for his health and our finances. If we'd count all the money he's spent on booze, we probably could be living high on the hog. We'd at least have the cash to fix the steps and rotten boards on the front porch.

DOUBLE TROUBLE AT THE PIONEER TUNNEL

Meemaw raises her lecture finger at Pop. Uh-oh. I think we're about to have World War III right here in the Leland kitchen.

"Thomas Leland," Meemaw says, "you know how I feel about your drinking. It's dangerous, I tell you. It's dangerous. And nothing but a big waste of money. Why, just yesterday I was reading in the book of Proverbs about alcohol and how it can mess up your mind. The two verses I remember the most sound something like this: 'Don't look upon wine when it is red, when it gives color in the cup, when it moves by itself. At the last, it bites like a serpent, and stings like a snake.' Tom—"

Pop releases an aggravated breath. "Mona, come on now. It's not that bad."

I bite my lip to keep from laughing. Wasn't he just talking about no aggravation at home?

"It's not that bad?" Meemaw says. "Who are you trying to kid?"

"Now, Mona," he fires out. "Don't get your dander up. I'm no town drunk. Just ask anybody. I just like a beer every now and then. There's no hurt to that. None at all."

"I've said my piece, Tom, and you know how I feel. And what do you think God thinks about all the money you've spent on booze when we ... oh, never mind." Meemaw's face turns bright red. She makes a beeline to her pork chops on the stove. "Just never mind."

"Pop," I say, "I sure wish you wouldn't—"

"Not you too," he says tongue-in-cheek. "My two favorite girls are ganging up on me."

"It's only because we care," Meemaw says over her shoulder as she turns the pork chops.

Pop wraps his arms around the boxes and struggles to pick them up. "Well, you two just never mind. You keep your religion to yourself, and I'll keep my booze to myself. Sounds like a good deal to me." He heads toward the door that opens to the cellar steps. "Pockets, get the door for me, and I'll pack these babies in a safe place downstairs."

"Sure, Pop." I open the door and feel like I'm an accessory to Pop's booze fest. Then I make up my mind to pray harder for him than I ever have before. And for Mom too.

I make a beeline to my bedroom, grab a pencil and some paper, and write a quick note to Mom. Anytime she writes to me, I make a point to get back to her right away, just so she knows I got her letter, and I'm still alive.

> Dear Mom,
>
> Thanks for the letter you just sent me. I always love hearing from you. I hope you can soon get the house painted and get rid of the "giant banana" look all over the place. I hope when you go on your vacation to New York City in the summer that you're able to stop by and see me. I miss you and would love to see you again. Aunt Alma too.
>
> Just in case you're wondering, I'm doing much better in school. Last marking period I got three A's, two B's, and a C in my worse subject, algebra. But that's better than last year when I was flunking math. Captain Ar and my friend Runner are both helping me with the math, and I'm trying real hard to get my grade up to a B.
>
> Well, I must leave now for the Salvation Army post. Captain Ar has given me and Runner an assignment. She's asked us to try and help two younger kids with their schoolwork in a special study period at the post on Mondays and Fridays.
>
> By the way, before I sign off, I want to share one of my favorite Bible verses with

you. Here it is. John 3:16, "For God so loved the world that he gave his only begotten son that whosoever believeth in him should not perish but have everlasting life." Mom, I pray for you all the time that you'll accept Jesus as your Savior. I want you to be in heaven with me some day.

    I LOVE YOU,
    Tommi Jo

    Friday night at six o'clock sharp, me and Runner have ourselves stationed in the post's game room, each of us at our own card table and with our own stack of books. Captain Ar had reminded us to have "lots to do" so we'd keep busy during this study period, all the while waiting for the Pawson brats to warm up to us, if they would at all.

    I'll have no trouble keeping busy. On Monday, I have to hand in a two-page report in history class about General Douglas McArthur, a big shot in World War II. I also have algebra homework, and for that I'll need some help from either Captain Ar or Runner. I know Runner gets A's in math, so we'll probably get our heads together over "x squared" in a little while.

    Earlier in her office, Captain Ar gave us a few last-minute instructions on how to handle the Pawsons over the next hour. She told us if Runner and I work together on any part of our homework, we should act like we're enjoying it but to do it for only a few minutes, not for the entire hour. Well, that's a no brainer for me. Anything I do with Runner would bring me the greatest pleasure. There's no acting like it's enjoyable for me. It's the real thing when I'm around him. I mean, it's hard to fake not having a racing heart and red-hot face when he gives me that sneaky wink every once in a while.

Anyway, Captain Ar said we shouldn't be discouraged if nothing happens tonight with the twins. She said to let them make the first move and to wait for them to ask us for help. She's with them in the office right now reading them the riot act and all the rules they're to follow.

This afternoon, Mr. Bill picked up the kids and their books at school, took the kids home to change out of their school clothes, and reminded them that he'd pick them up at five-thirty, so they should be coming into the game room any minute.

Captain Ar's door opens, and in come Mr. Bill, the twins, and Captain Ar. Mr. Bill heads for the kitchenette in the back of the room where he'll be getting snacks ready for Fun Night and "keeping his eye on things" for the next hour.

The twins actually look like they might have taken a bath and put clean clothes on sometime during the past week. Dale's got a faded red T-shirt on, wrinkled but clean, and Gail's T-shirt is the color of grass. They both have wrinkled blue jeans on with the knees out, but, at least, the jeans look clean too. And their hair even looks shiny and neat. I wouldn't be a bit surprised if Captain Ar braided Gail's pigtails and Mr. Bill trimmed Dale's hair a little. The kids almost look cute ... except for their freckled faces. They're both hanging on pouts that could stop a clock.

"Dale," Captain Ar says, "I'd like you to sit over there." She points to a card table near where Runner is stationed. "And, Gail, you sit at that one." She points to the table next to the one where I'm sitting.

"Hi, kids," Runner says.

"Hi," I say and give a quick wave.

"I'm sure you remember Pockets and Runner, don't you?" Captain Ar says to the twins.

The two just scowl as they walk to their tables and plop their books down.

DOUBLE TROUBLE AT THE PIONEER TUNNEL

"Excuse me?" Captain Ar says. "I didn't hear what either of you said."

"Yeah," Dale spits out. "Hi."

"Hi." Gail never looks at either Runner or me.

"So," Captain Ar says, "this hour will fly by, and I hope you can get most, if not all, of your homework done. It's Fun Night time at seven o'clock, so the study period will end shortly before that."

"Can we stay for that?" Dale asks as he slumps into his chair.

"Now, Dale," Captain Ar says, "you already know the answer to that. You have to earn your way back to Fun Night. You behave yourselves, and in no time flat, you'll be back here. But tonight Mr. Bill will take you home after the study period ends."

I rivet my stare on both kids, waiting for a smart-aleck remark or maybe a tantrum explosion, but neither kid says boo. Gail flops in her chair and under her breath says, "This whole thing makes me sick."

"Excuse me?" Captain Ar says to her. "Gail, did you say something? I didn't quite hear it."

"No," Gail says, and flops open a book. "It's nothing."

"Oh, and remember," Captain Ar adds, "your teachers have given me all your homework assignments, so I know what needs to be done. And if you don't get it done, you also know what that means, don't you?" She crosses her arms and waits.

I'd love to know what "that means" means.

"Yeah," the twins say almost in unison. "We know."

Captain Ar turns toward her office. "I'll be working at my desk if anyone needs anything. I'll see you all in an hour." She leaves and positions her office door open with just a slight crack.

I glance at Mr. Bill, and he's busy as a beaver, but I know he'll have one eye on us the whole time.

I look at Runner who gives me a subtle smile then settles in at his table, opens a book, and grabs his pencil and notebook.

I settle at my table and open my algebra. Out of the corner of my eye I watch the twins as they slump in their seats. Almost in unison they grab a book from their pile, flop the book open, and bury their faces in their books. It looks like they don't plan to move another muscle for the whole next hour.

I tackle my math, but it doesn't take long for x squared to unravel my brain. "Runner," I say, "can I see you about my algebra?"

"Sure," he says. "Come on over."

Runner is a whiz at math. He's so good, I know he can help me with my algebra. In way too short a time with his "instruction," including a few really dumb jokes and laughter, I get my x squared. Out of the corner of my eye, I watch Dale, who looks like he's studying hard but, out of the corner of his eye, is watching every move we make. I head back to my table and tackle my history report.

In about ten minutes, Runner pushes his algebra book aside, grabs his English text, and joins me. "Hey, Pockets, how about a little help with diagramming."

Well, I almost burst out laughing. Me help Runner? With English?

First of all, he's a grade ahead of me. Second, he gets good grades in English too. Third, after nine years of school, it's just starting to sink into me that English is the language Americans speak, so I should learn it. "You're kidding," I say to him. "You want me to help you with diagramming? I don't think so."

"Okay then. I have a test on Monday on the parts of speech." He pulls out a paper from his English book. "How about giving me a review of all the definitions."

"Sure, I'll do anything to help you," I say.

DOUBLE TROUBLE AT THE PIONEER TUNNEL

As Runner joins me, out of the corner of my eye, I watch Gail, who looks like she's studying hard, but out of the corner of her eye she's watching every move we make.

After about fifteen minutes of English review including more dumb jokes, Runner heads back to his table.

The rest of the study period is as boring as a 1930s movie about Marie Antoinette. I get most of my report written, and I can see Runner has finished his homework and is reading *The Lion, the Witch, and the Wardrobe*. I glance at Dale, who's still staring at the same book he started with and not moving a muscle. Gail's the same.

I glance at the wall clock. Ten minutes to seven. It looks like me and Runner have scored a big, fat zero with the twins. I look at Runner, who just shrugs then starts packing his books.

I do the same when, out of the blue, I feel a tap on my shoulder.

I turn, and there stands Gail.

"D-Do you know I'm twelve-and-a-half years old?" she squeaks out.

I feel like screaming at the top of my lungs, "Yes. And your birthday's in July!" But I just smile at her and say, "Yes, and you'll soon be a teenager like the rest of us here at the post."

"S-Sounds like you're really lousy at math," she says, "but how are you with science? What do you know about the planets?"

At quarter after seven, as soon as me and Runner—Runner says the correct English is "Runner and I"—grab our hot dogs, cupcakes, and soda from the line-up of snacks, Captain Ar asks us to join her in her office while the other kids, minus the twins, scarf down their food and play games. We flop in the chairs in front of her desk, and as we gobble down our food, she relaxes in her chair and sips on a cup of coffee. I know it's coffee, because her whole office smells like coffee beans.

"Well," she says, "it looks like you two made it to first base with the twins. At least, you did, Pockets."

I swallow a bite of hot dog then say, "I can't believe it. They hardly moved a muscle the whole hour. But just as we were getting packed up to leave, Gail asked me for help. But with only a few minutes left, there wasn't much I could do. And she had to remind me again that she's twelve-and-a half years old. She drives me crazy with that!"

Runner adds, "And Dale hardly looked my way at all. He had his nose buried in a book the whole time. But once or twice I heard him say under his breath, "Aw rats." I peeked and noticed he was working on his math, so he must be pretty lousy with that. But did he come to me for help? No way."

"But that first move by Gail is a milestone, believe me," Captain Ar says, pointing at me. "It's a great start."

I say, "The funny thing about it is Gail wanted me to tell her jokes more than help her with her science. That cracked me up."

"So," Captain Ar says, "both of you should have an arsenal of jokes lined up for the next time. I can see with their sad lives that they'd gravitate toward anything that would make them smile. And Gail's obsession with her birthday, really both their birthdays, is a given. I'll place a very safe bet that those two have never, ever had a party. When June rolls around, we'll give them the party of their lives."

I count six months away on my fingers. "Now wait a minute. Gail said she's twelve-and-a-half. That takes us to July, doesn't it?"

DOUBLE TROUBLE AT THE PIONEER TUNNEL

"Not really," Captain Ar says. "I've checked her records, and their birthday isn't in July. She just says she's twelve-and-a-half no matter what time of the year it is after six months have passed."

"So, when is it?" Runner asks.

"June," Captain Ar says and gives me a got-cha smile. "June 28."

My mouth drops open and gets stuck until I get my brain unscrambled. "June 28? That's my birthday!"

Now Runner's mouth is stuck in neutral. Then he says, "That's right. It is!"

"Well," Captain Ar says, "aren't we going to have a grand time on June 28?"

I just give the woman a disgusted look. "Yeah, right."

"Now," she says, "let's get back to the task at hand and how well you two did with them tonight."

"I'm sure they still have a pile of homework to do," Runner says. "I never saw Dale do anything but stare at one book."

"Me neither with Gail," I say.

"Oh, you'll be surprised to hear they got almost all their homework done," Captain Ar says. "I checked the work they finished before they left. They were busier than you thought when you two were focusing on your own assignments. When I praised them for working so hard, they acted like they didn't care two hoots that they got so much done, but I could tell how pleased they were. I've told you I believe they're quite intelligent, but no one has ever made them do their schoolwork. With our monitoring their progress, their grades should certainly improve, and that can only help how they feel about themselves."

"This might be easier than we thought," I say. "I can't wait until Monday to see what happens."

"We better spruce up on our jokes," Runner says. "How about this one …

Last night at supper I asked my dad, 'Are caterpillars good to eat?'

Dad said, 'No. Why would you ask a question like that?'

I said, 'Well, there was one in your salad, but it's gone now.'"

We burst out laughing, then Captain Ar says, "That's a good one, Runner, so both of you look for a few more jokes like that. But concerning how *easy* this could be with the twins? Hold on now. The strong-will battle with these two hasn't been won in a long shot. You had a small victory tonight, but with the twins, you can't count on anything. Just remember, they're schemers, and they're experts at lying as a self-defense mechanism. Those two run completely on their emotions, and if things aren't going well at home, and most of the time they're not, they'll release that tension, anxiety, and fear in all different ways. It might be tantrums, destructive behavior like you saw at the park, or they might withdraw into stubborn silence. All I can tell you to do is always be on guard. They could be sweet as sugar pie one minute, and the next minute they could be ready to give you a black eye."

"Or a big gooney on your shin," I say.

"Yeah," Runner says. "I'll never forget how quick things got ugly here with them wanting to shoot pool."

"My shin is still black and blue," I say. "I haven't forgotten either."

"Patience, persistence, and prayer, you two," Captain Ar says. "It'll take a while, but let's see what God can do with Dale and Gail. This is a really tough case because of the situation with their parents. I know if the kids could get to church, that would help tremendously, but with their mother being so sick most of the time and their dad ... well, it's not going to happen. I'd love to take them with me to church, but sometimes I get called to emergencies, and I'd have no one to watch them if I'd have to leave in a hurry."

"I wish we could get them to our church," I say. "But me and Meemaw—Runner says the correct English is 'Meemaw and I'—walk to church. Pop's not in the church-going mode in his life yet, and he comes in so late on Saturday nights, we can't count on him driving us the six blocks, so we walk."

"Hey!" Runner snaps his fingers. "I can ask my folks if they'd pick them up. The Pawsons' house isn't that far out of the way for us to get them. I don't know how Mom will feel about it, especially since she knows all about the twins. I've been filling my parents in on everything that's been going on. All I can do is ask."

Captain Ar breaks out into one of her best smiles, the kind that lights up the whole room. "Runner, that's wonderful. You do that and let me know what your parents say. God only knows how badly these children and their parents need the Lord in their lives. If it works out for you to pick them up, you can consider yourself a junior missionary!"

Runner and I look at each other, and we both break into smiles almost matching Captain Ar's.

CHAPTER SEVEN

The next Friday night at the post turns into a triple knock-your-socks-off time.

First of all, during our six o'clock study period with the twins, we finally make some progress, which is a thousand times better than last Monday. They didn't say boo then to either of us for the whole hour. But now, Gail actually lets me help her with English and science for a good half hour, the whole time acting like she hates every minute of it, except when I throw in a dumb joke. Then she forces out a pathetic giggle.

Runner makes progress too. He spends a good amount of time helping Dale, while the kid hangs a pout on his face that looks like he's being bitten by a tarantula. But, at least, the kid finally warms up to Runner. That's knock-your-socks-off number one.

Next, when all the other kids arrive at seven for Fun Night, the twins don't leave. That's knock-your-socks-off number two. Captain Ar pulls Runner and me aside and tells us she's allowing Gail and Dale to stay tonight for two reasons.

First, they've been behaving in their counseling sessions with her, and Mr. Dimock, the school principal, told Captain Ar he's noticed a slight improvement in their attitude and conduct.

The second reason the twins could stay turns out to be the third knock-your-socks-off surprise for every one of us.

DOUBLE TROUBLE AT THE PIONEER TUNNEL

It's seven-thirty, and while the other kids are having a blast, I'm playing Uncle Wiggly with Gail, who looks like she's bored to death. I'm sure I look the same because I *am* bored to death. And she told me for the zillionth time she's twelve-and-a-half years old! She's gonna drive me crazy with that.

Coochie, Trudy, Reuben, and Leona are shooting pool, and it's killing me to be sitting here babysitting. I glance to the other side of the room where Runner is playing checkers with Dale, and both of them look like they're having a race to see who can look bored the most.

In the back corner, I spot Moose with two new boys I haven't met yet. Yes! Moose is here shooting darts with them. I'm not really surprised to see him because I know he's had a lot of counseling with Captain Ar, so he obviously has behaved himself enough to make it here tonight. I would love to have been a little mouse and heard that first counseling session he had with her. I bet it didn't take her long to put Mr. Super Jock in his place.

Now, about knock-your-socks-off number three! Every kid who's been coming to the post the last year gets their socks knocked off. Guess who walks in the game room with Captain Ar.

Yup. Ruth McGinnis!

"Look who came for a visit," Captain Ar says, her smile lighting up the entire room.

All the kids who had met Miss McGinnis a few months back in Honesdale at the town's brand new poolroom stand at attention like she's some kind of royalty. Well, in a way she is. In the game of pool world, she's known as the Queen of Billiards, and can she ever shoot pool. The last time we saw her, she told us she has run off over a hundred balls without missing one single shot. And she's done it many times.

"Hi, kids!" she says.

She looks like a real winner with her dark hair in a plain-Jane short, wavy style and her snappy clothes. Her thin figure touts one of the coolest outfits I've ever seen. She's wearing a white blouse with big polka dots that look like pool balls, a black straight skirt, and black shoes with thick soles and ties—the kind of shoes Captain Ar wears all the time. Miss McGinnis is also carrying her pool stick in a black leather case.

We who know the wonder woman rush to her side and greet her. I glance back and see Gail, Dale, Moose, and the two other newbies who don't know beans about pool or Miss McGinnis. All their faces are draped in a "big deal" grouchy face. If they only knew. I think they're about to find out.

"How are you all?" Miss McGinnis says as we crowd around her. "And, Pockets, how's your game?"

My face heats up ten degrees. "Good, ma'am. Real good."

"Well, you keep at it," she says, "and one day you'll be a champion too."

If she only knew that was my dream just a little while back. Then I met Captain Ar, and everything in my life changed.

"Kids," Captain Ar says, "Miss McGinnis called me last week and told me she'd be shooting in a billiard competition in Maryland today. She asked if she could stop by this evening on her way home and shoot some pool with you. Now how could I refuse that?"

"Did you win the competition?" I ask her. "And were other girls shooting?" I think I detect a slight blush on Miss McGinnis's cheeks.

"Well," she says, "if you must know, I took first place in eight ball. And, no, there were all men competing against me."

Amidst a barrage of smiles, applause, and wows, I glance back and see the newbies have joined the group.

DOUBLE TROUBLE AT THE PIONEER TUNNEL

All of them but the twins have changed their look, now anxious to see Miss McGinnis in action.

Gail and Dale? Standing with their arms folded, both of them still have that nasty "big deal" look plastered all over their faces.

Captain Ar takes a few steps to a small table against the wall and picks up a glass jar about the size of a football with tiny, folded papers in it. "Kids, would any of you like to shoot a game of eight ball with Miss McGinnis?"

"Are you kidding?" Runner says.

"For real?" Reuben adds while practically everyone else says yes or nods with smiles from ear to ear.

Captain Ar raises the jar and takes off the lid. "Kids, your names are all in here on these pieces of paper. We're going to draw three names, and those three will each shoot a game of eight ball with Miss McGinnis."

"Oh, wow!" Trudy yells, her chipmunk cheeks fiery red. "How cool is that? I hope you pick me."

A chorus of "Me too!" rings out.

"I'll ask Miss McGinnis to pick the winners." Captain Ar holds the jar.

Miss McGinnis pulls out three papers. "The winners are Reuben, Coochie, and Pockets."

"Yahoo!" I yell.

"Aw right!" Reuben and Coochie say while everyone else moans.

"But I've seen her shoot," Coochie throws in. "We won't even get a shot."

"Oh," Miss McGinnis says, "I'll have mercy on you. You'll get at least one shot."

Everyone laughs.

"Now," Captain Ar says, "before we start the games, we're going to pull three more names."

"Three more?" Leona asks. "Why?"

"Now remember," Captain Ar says, "we're all going to snow camp in northeastern Pennsylvania in a few weeks.

I should say all of you who walk the straight and narrow will earn the privilege to go. Then on our way home, we'll stop in Honesdale at the poolroom and see Miss McGinnis again. Well, she's agreed to play three more of you in eight ball then, so we're going to draw three more names right now for those winners."

"So," I say, "we can't win twice. Can we?"

"I'm afraid not," Miss McGinnis says. She pulls out three names and reads them. "The winners are Moose, Trudy, and Gail."

Moose and Trudy explode with excitement. The others hang pouts all over their bodies.

I turn toward Gail, and she has the surprise of a lifetime on her face, kind of like she just won a million bucks. Or maybe that she turned thirteen early!

"Me?" she says. "I don't know nuttin' about shooting pool."

"Miss McGinnis will teach you, Gail," Captain Ar says. "This is really something special you can work for."

Gail just shrugs and hangs kind of a "who cares" pout on her face, one that looks like she's trying her very best to hold back a smile.

I glance at Dale, and he just shrugs with another "big deal" look. I'm sure he was whispering "aw rats" under his breath.

The next hour proves to be one of the best times in my life. Miss McGinnis plays us three winners, and although she wins every game, I know she deliberately misses easy shots so we have the chance to shoot. I wouldn't have cared if she had run off every single ball, and I would have never gotten a shot. I just love to watch her shoot. Then after the three games of eight ball, she also shows us some awesome trick shots while we have our snack Mr. Bill had prepared.

I could be wrong on this one, but while we all munch and watch Miss McGinnis, I think I actually see a new look on both the twins' faces. Gail's eyes are almost as big as ping-pong balls, and she never takes her stare away from the female pool shark. I don't know how Gail does it, but, somehow, she manages another stingy smile while scarfing down two pieces of pizza.

And Dale? For the first time, he also watches Miss McGinnis with googly eyes and a smile that just seems to be forcing itself out.

I'll bet the socks I got knocked off me tonight that these twins are going to try their best to earn the privilege to go on the snow camp trip. I might as well make up my mind that they're going and plan a "buddy strategy" instead of wishing they can't go.

I glance at Runner, and the look on his face tells me he's thinking exactly the same thing.

The next week or so proves to be a roller coaster ride with the twins.

Runner's parents pick up the twins and take them to church the next two Sundays. During the preaching service, I keep a keen eye on the twins. With Gail sandwiched between Runner's dad and mom and Dale sandwiched between Runner and Mr. Ramsey, the little terrors don't say boo during the service. Dale even falls asleep halfway through the preaching part. The way they all look kind of reminds me of prisoners with armed guards. And I feel sorry for the twins because of the way they're dressed. They're wearing the same clothes they wore to the study periods last Monday and Friday. I bet they don't even have a set of "good" clothes.

That's the "up" part of the roller coaster ride. But the two little monsters hit rock bottom in school.

Before the next Friday evening's study period, Captain Ar tells Runner and me that the twins didn't do their homework from Tuesday to Thursday, just because they "didn't want to." She also tells us she read them the riot act. They will make up all the homework, or they will *not* be going to snow camp, which is coming up next weekend. I know it's wrong the way I feel, but I hope they don't get it all done.

Now it's Monday afternoon and me and Runner just finish the hour's study time with the twins. They work their little tails off, finishing almost all of last week's late assignments. I feel like sabotaging Gail's math so she turns in pages of homework with all wrong answers, but then I ask God to forgive me for my selfishness and help Gail get everything done right.

Does she even throw a thanks my way when we finish? No way. She just reminds me how old she is. But Captain Ar says if we do anything for the Lord, we shouldn't always be looking for a thank you from anyone else.

So, I'm on my way home from the post, all the way contemplating Captain Ar's words of wisdom. I just hope someday when I'm old like her that I can think through things and do what God would want me to do and not always do what I want to do.

I rush into my house, throw my books on the sofa, and hurry to the kitchen. At this time of day, I can always count on Meemaw cooking up something yummy.

Surprise! Pop's sitting at the kitchen table and sipping a bottle of beer. I glance at the clock—Four-thirty. This time of the day he's usually spending his overtime earnings at Malloney's. Meemaw is at the stove, warming leftovers from Sunday's dinner, chicken corn soup. I can smell the delicious aroma.

DOUBLE TROUBLE AT THE PIONEER TUNNEL

"Pop," I say, "what are you doing home so soon? Are you sick or something?" After I say that, I wish I could eat my words. I want him to know I'm really glad to see him at this time of day.

"You'll see more of me at suppertime," Pop says. "I have had it with Malloney's. That darn Pawson started his antics again today. I almost gave him a knuckle sandwich, but I just told him to shut the hole in his face and left."

I'm so happy that Pop's going to be home more often that I could do cartwheels. But I can't figure out why he doesn't claim another bar as his hangout. There must be at least five more booze joints in Ashland. Well, I for one will never, ever bring up those options. "Pop, it's great that you're planning to spend more time at home. Isn't that great, Meemaw?" I rush to the fridge, pull out a bottle of orange soda, and join Pop at the table.

"Absolutely," she says as she stirs the soup. "Now I can plan my meals and the time we can all eat together."

"Meemaw, do you wanna hear about my day? Pop, how about you?"

Pop just shrugs and throws me a stingy smile. "Anything exciting happen?"

"Sure," Meemaw says. "How did your study period go with the twins?" She brings three soup bowls and silverware to the table and sets our places.

"Not too bad. Captain Ar had laid down the law before the session started. So, the Pawsons were pretty much civilized. And I had told you they didn't do any of their homework for three days last week, so they worked their little buns off in the study time today. I know they want to go to snow camp, and I also think they're realizing that Captain Ar means what she says, and if they goof up one more time, they will *not* be going with us."

"Speaking of the Pawsons," Meemaw says, "that reminds me. Pastor Sutcliff asked to talk to Pauline Ramsey and me after the church service yesterday morning. He had met the twins earlier that morning and said he'd like us two gals to spearhead a drive to help the family. He said he's going to visit their home this week and get to know the parents. I told him all I know about Hattie and Parnell, which wasn't very much nor very good. I haven't seen Hattie in years, and I'm not really sure what keeps her bedridden most of the time. And Parnell—"

"Give me the preacher's phone number," Pop practically yells, "and I'll tell him all about the louse."

"Now, Tom," Meemaw says, carrying her pot of soup to the table. "Church is just what the man needs. Don't you think?"

"And a swift kick in the pants too," Pop says then finishes his bottle of beer.

The way Pop's talking, he has a snoot full, and the way I see it, he needs a lot of church and a swift kick himself.

"Gee, Meemaw," I say, "what are you going to do to help the Pawsons?"

"Well, Pauline and I are going to get together sometime this week and plan. For one thing, we're going to have the church members send in meals a few times a week for quite a while, and we're going to see about getting some decent clothes for those poor kids. They look like little homeless ragamuffins."

"If they had a decent father who'd provide for them, they wouldn't need all that help," Pop says.

"Tom," Meemaw says, "it's our job as Christians to help those in need." She grabs a cup of coffee and joins us at the table. "I'm praying that the love our church shows to that family will bring Parnell to the Lord. God can change anyone's heart, but it has to start with us showing him the love of Christ."

"Hmmph," Pop said. "But some people are hopeless."

"Are you hopeless, Pop?" The words just slipped out of my mouth, and I swallowed hard.

DOUBLE TROUBLE AT THE PIONEER TUNNEL

Pop stared at me with a look I have never seen on his face before. Ever. Like I had just slapped him in the face.

I stared back, not sure what to say, and no one moved a muscle ... until Meemaw finally said, "The soup's getting cold. Let's pray and dig in."

CHAPTER EIGHT

After helping Meemaw with the supper dishes, I crash on my bed and tackle my homework. But as usual, when I try to do stupid algebra, my mind wanders, and I think about my mom and pop, and the floodgates in my eyes bust wide open.

Why can't we be a happy family, living together in one house? But then I remember what Captain Ar always tells me, and lickety split, the floodgates slam shut and dry up the tears, and I feel like I'm getting a grip on life and the way it is, not the way I think it should be.

"Pockets," she says, "you just keep praying for them. You might never be one happy family again, but I believe you've come to know what's most important is their relationship with God. If you can't talk to them about your faith, may I suggest you write them letters with Bible verses. God's Word can sink into the hardest of hearts. You never know how God can use one of your letters to soften your parents' attitude about the Lord."

I push the books aside and pull out my notebook, paper, and pen. I pull out Mom's letter from the notebook and read the letter. I write a short note to her, then I do something I've never done before. I write a letter to my dad.

> Dear Pop,
> I want to write and tell you I'm sorry if I hurt your feelings tonight at supper when I asked you if you're hopeless. I didn't mean anything

by it. In fact, I try very hard to respect you all the time because I love you very much.

I love you so much that I want you to be in heaven with me and Meemaw someday. I know that doesn't mean anything to you now, and you don't want to hear about Jesus, but I have to tell you how much he means to me and how he's helped me straighten out my messed-up life.

Thanks to Captain Ar, I have learned to read the Bible, and it has tons of verses that have helped me. I want to tell you about the most important ones. Here they are.

"For God so loved the world, that he gave his only begotten Son, that whosoever believeth in him should not perish, but have everlasting life." That verse is John 3:16.

Romans 6:23 says, "For the wages of sin is death; but the gift of God is eternal life through Jesus Christ our Lord."

Pop, when Captain Ar explained these verses to me, for the first time ever I understood what it meant to give my heart, my life, to God. When I did that, I felt completely different deep inside. You can see how I've changed, and I don't get in a lot of trouble anymore. It's because God helps me keep on the straight and narrow. If I can learn to control my big mouth, I'll feel like God really has performed a miracle in my life.

All I'm trying to say is you'd be a lot happier if you'd give your heart to God. Meemaw also did that a while back, and I'm sure you can see a difference in her too.

We both love you very much. I hope you don't get mad because I wrote you this letter.

I've been wanting to tell you for a long time how I feel and that I love you.

    So does God, more than anybody.

    Your daughter,

    Pockets

I jump off the bed and pull two envelopes and one stamp out of my desk drawer. You talk about a miracle! It's a miracle I can find those things right away, but lately I've been keeping one drawer neat for important things like envelopes and stamps. Forget the other drawers.

I address Mom's envelope, and after writing "Pop" on the other envelope, I think about how to give him the letter. I know he's downstairs in the living room reading the newspaper, but I chicken out taking it right to him. I decide to sneak it in the pocket of the coat he wears to work every day. That way I'm positive he'll see it.

Satisfied with my plan, I flop on the bed and tackle that nasty algebra again.

It's Thursday evening, and before I blab about the super weekend just ahead, I'll mention that Pop never said boo about my letter. Maybe it dropped out of his pocket, and he never saw it. Now I wish I had handed the letter to him. Maybe I'll write him another one in a while.

Anyway, it's the start of the second weekend in February, and three inches of snow just blanketed practically the whole state of Pennsylvania. Perfect for snow camp!

How can you have snow camp without snow? I was thinking all week if we didn't get any fresh snow, we'd be going to "mud camp."

Most of us counselees are at the post with Captain Ar and Mr. Bill. There are nine of us kids here—Me, Runner,

DOUBLE TROUBLE AT THE PIONEER TUNNEL

my best friend Leona, Coochie, Trudy, Reuben, Moose, and the twins. Boomer and Nick, the other two new kids, goofed big-time this past week and can't go. I have no idea what they did, or didn't do, but it must have been major because they aren't here.

So, the rest of us are here on Thursday, not Friday as usual, because tomorrow at the crack of dawn, we're leaving for snow camp, and we won't be back until late Saturday night.

I'm about ready to jump out of my skin with excitement despite the fact that the twins earned the right to go. I can't imagine how I'm going to tolerate two whole days of babysitting the brats. I must admit they're doing a little better lately, but I'm sure that was all just a big act so they could go on the trip. Especially Gail since she won the chance to play a game of eight ball with Miss McGinnis when we go the poolroom in Honesdale on our way home.

Mr. Bill had just served us barbecue, chips, pumpkin donuts, and cocoa, so we're sitting in a circle and munching on our food while we listen to Captain Ar give us the details about the trip.

Runner is sitting next to me, so I have to try to be cool and not be so obvious when I want to stare into his gorgeous, chocolate-brown eyes. It's really hard, though, when I have to shift my eyes at a sharp right-angled turn to sneak a look. After I do that, I gaze around the circle at the kids, and they're all bug-eyed and hanging on the edge of their seats listening to Captain Ar while they're stuffing their mouths with food. Gail and Dale, one on each side of her, even have an almost eager look.

I study the twins from head to toe, and the first thing I notice is they're wearing different clothes. Clean clothes. Some even look new. Bright orange sweatshirts, blue jeans, and new white sneakers. On the backs of their chairs the twins had hung what look like brand-new winter jackets. Gail's coat is bright red, and Dale's is a shiny black material. Both coats have fur-lined hoods. I bet they have new boots for the trip too. And the twins both seem like they're trying real hard to smile, but their faces won't let them.

As I stare, I remember back to yesterday when Meemaw said that Mrs. Sutcliff had gone shopping for some clothes for the kids, and tonight, Captain Ar told me and Runner that someone had donated enough money to get the twins new coats. I wouldn't be a bit surprised to find out that Captain Ar bought the coats. That's just the way she is. Always ready to give, give, give.

I can't take my stare away from Gail and Dale, thinking maybe they're finally feeling some love from Captain Ar and the church folk. Maybe even from me and Runner? I wonder if some new, clean clothes have given those poor kids a feeling they *are* wanted, or, at least, liked by somebody, and they don't have to act crazy to get attention.

That thought takes me back to the beginning of my school year when Meemaw bought me some new clothes, including a black pullover sweater with rhinestones decorating the neckline, a blue poodle skirt, and brown and white saddle shoes. Gone were the days of wearing the same old worn-out blouses and skirts from the thrift store. I felt like a million bucks walking into my homeroom the first day. I bet that's how those twins feel right about now.

"Kids," Captain Ar says, "we need to go over all the rules, so get ready." She passes around a small stack of papers. "Take one of these. All you need to know is on the paper."

Everyone takes a paper, glances at it, and looks back at Captain Ar.

"I am very proud of you," she says. "You all remembered to get your parents to sign the permission slips to go on the trip, and you all got your school principals to sign the release forms to be off school tomorrow. Good for you!

DOUBLE TROUBLE AT THE PIONEER TUNNEL

Now remember you need to be here at eight o'clock sharp tomorrow morning. And we plan to return by eight on Saturday evening, so you can get settled at home before it's too late." Captain Ar gives us one of her sly looks. "And you who go to church regularly won't have an I'm-too-tired excuse to miss on Sunday morning."

Everyone breaks out with a smile. Even Gail and Dale! I didn't think the twins' faces knew how to do that!

"Now," Captain Ar says, "let's look at the paper I just gave you. We have some very, very important rules on there that all of you need to obey. The rules aren't to take away your fun. They're to keep all of us safe."

I glance at the paper and there are five "rules" we're to follow. I wonder what the woman will do if someone breaks one of these. I'm thinking we probably won't be there an hour, and the twins will have broken all of them. I take a deep breath and get ready for her to read us the riot act.

Captain Ar says, "Number one, and most important of all, when we get to the camp and get settled in our chalets, you are to never go anywhere on the campgrounds alone."

"What's a chah-let?" Trudy asks.

"It's pronounced shah-lay," Captain Ar says. "It's a small cottage, like a bunkhouse where we'll all be sleeping. Mr. Bill will be with the boys in one chalet, and I'll be with all of you girls in another one. I'm assuming we won't be the only group there for the two days, so it'll be important to remember which chalets are ours. They're probably numbered to make it easier for us to find the one we're staying in. In the brochure about the camp, it says there are ten chalets, five for boys, and five for girls, so this sounds like a pretty big place."

"I hope nobody else shows up," Moose blurts out. "Then we'll have everything to ourselves."

"Well," Coochie chimes in, "that's a pretty selfish attitude. I'd like to meet some other kids and make some new friends, especially the girls." He peaks his eyebrows several times and shows every tooth in his mouth with a dimpled smile.

"All right, all right, you two," Captain Ar says. "Time will tell if we're the only group there or not. But I think as popular as this place is by the looks of the brochure, there should be other groups there too."

"Are we allowed to talk to other kids who might be there?" I ask.

"Sure," Captain Ar says. "We'll get to that in a minute. Let's look at rule number two. Stay with our group unless you ask permission to do something different from what we're doing. Here's an example. If we're all sledding but you'd like to go ice skating, first of all, you need to ask Mr. Bill or me for permission. And then you must have a buddy from our group to go with you."

I glance at the twins, and both of them are slouching in their chairs with disgust draped all over their faces. They're probably wondering if they're going to have any fun at all ... without breaking any of the rules.

"Rule number three," Captain Ar says, "is no griping or complaining, especially with each other or to the camp staff. The workers there will be doing their best to help you have the time of your life. If you have something that doesn't suit you, just come to me, and we'll sit down and discuss it. One rotten apple can spoil the whole bunch. I think you all know what that means."

Leona brushes her wavy hair back off her eyebrow. "Yeah, it means if you hang around complainers, you'll become one."

"That's right," Captain Ar says. "But to tell you the truth, I haven't heard much complaining from any of you in this group, and I'm proud of you for that."

I glance at Moose then zero in on Runner, and I know just what Runner's thinking. *She doesn't know Moose like we know him.*

DOUBLE TROUBLE AT THE PIONEER TUNNEL

"Rule number four," Captain Ar, says. "You were all asked to bring five dollars spending money, if you wanted to. Although all your meals are covered with your registration fee, they have a snack bar and a little gift shop there, and I found out they have a pool table, and you have to put a quarter in a coin slot on the camp's table to play. So ... use your money wisely. If you blow it all on Friday, under no circumstances are you to ask anyone else in our group for any to get you through Saturday."

And I bet my booties that Captain Ar will make sure the twins have a little spending money. We'll see how far that goes.

Runner raises his hand. "We won't need to unload our pool sticks at the camp, will we?"

"No," Captain Ar says. "We'll leave them packed until we get to Honesdale and the Hot Shot Pool Room. Knowing pool tables as I do, I'm assuming the table at camp is smaller than ours, probably only about a three-foot by six-foot. And I think you all are going to be so busy with the other activities, you might not have time for pool."

"What time are we getting there?" Coochie asks.

"My ETA at camp is eleven a.m.," Captain Ar says. "And we need to be in Honesdale by two o'clock on Saturday. Even though the camp has activities planned all Saturday afternoon, we'll leave there right after lunch to get to Honesdale. Miss McGinnis will be waiting for us at the poolroom. That will give us about three hours to spend with her before we head home."

"I can't decide which is more exciting, the camp or shooting pool with that pool shark," Reuben says.

"Me neither," I say. "Even though I don't get to shoot with her in Honesdale, I just love to watch her shoot. She is awesome!"

"All right, let's get back on track here," Captain Ar says, her blue eyes sparkling and her smile lighting up the whole room. "We've got only one more rule to review.

Kids, please be kind to one another and be very courteous to other kids and to the staff at the camp. You who are Christians know how important it is to share your faith in a subtle but friendly way."

"What if somebody's rude to us?" Reuben asks.

"Do *not* take it into your own hands," Captain Ar says. "You come to Mr. Bill or me, and we'll discuss it. The last thing we need at a Christian camp is a fight or even hard feelings."

"Got-cha," Reuben says.

Runner raises his hand.

"Yes, Runner?" Captain Ar says.

"What if ... what if someone breaks any of these rules? What then?"

"I'm glad you asked," Captain Ar says tongue-in-cheek. "Here's the deal. We certainly can't send the rule breaker home, and we're certainly not going to penalize the entire group for one person's disobedience and pack up and all go home. But if anyone does break a rule or get in any kind of trouble, he or she will spend a lot of time right by my side or with Mr. Bill. While everyone else is having fun, you'll be sitting with one of us and just watching. Depending on the infraction, it could be an hour, several hours, or the rest of the time we're at the camp."

"Wow," Trudy says, her chipmunk cheeks fiery red. "I can't imagine spending hours sitting and just watching everyone else having fun. You can count on me to keep every rule and then some."

"Me too," most of the kids add.

I glance at the twins, and I've seen that look on their faces before. In fact, I'm sure I've had that look on my face in algebra class. Their eyes are staring off into space, and I'd bet my best wooden nickel they haven't heard a word of what was said the last five minutes.

"Does anyone feel like we're taking you off to prison instead of to camp?" Captain Ar asks with her smile.

DOUBLE TROUBLE AT THE PIONEER TUNNEL

We all raise our hands and smile back. Except the twins. They sit with their arms folded and their thoughts in La La Land.

"But," I say, "we wouldn't mind as long as you and Mr. Bill would be our prison wardens."

"And," Runner adds, "if there's a pool table in the clink."

Everyone but the twins burst out laughing.

The twins' spaceship lands from La La Land, and they look around, their faces reflecting their thoughts, figuring they missed something really good.

"So," Captain Ar says, "there you have it. To be honest with you all, this list is not bad at all. It's really no different from the rules we have here at the post with the exception of wandering off and having to pay for pool table time. Speaking of pool table time, finish your snacks, and let the games begin!"

CHAPTER NINE

It's Friday morning, and we're just about there!

Since there are eleven of us, Captain Ar had to rent a used Volkswagen van from a car dealer in Ashland. She said there's no way we could all squeeze into the post's small, beat-up station wagon, especially with Runner, Reuben, and Moose—three big guys—trying to fit in.

In the Volkswagen, Captain Ar had given us all assigned seats with Mr. Bill sitting all the way in the back with Reuben and Coochie. Gail with brand-new clothes and boots is up in the front seat, and the rest of us have filled in the other seats with Dale in brand-new clothes and boots squeezed between Runner and Moose.

It takes us three hours to get to the Marching Forward Camp in Wayne County. That's because we had to make two pit stops for the twins, who said they "couldn't wait any longer." I think they were just bored and wanted to do something other than stare out the windows. I know Captain Ar had her eye on them the whole time at the gas stations' candy shelves. And in the van, they hardly said boo except when the rest of us told a round of ridiculous jokes. Then they actually laughed out loud. Oh, and Gail made a point to tell us a half dozen times that she's twelve-and-a-half. We're so sick of hearing it, we're all about ready to dropkick her to the moon.

DOUBLE TROUBLE AT THE PIONEER TUNNEL

The sun is splitting a crystal-clear blue sky as we pull into the campgrounds. Right off the bat, I notice the camp had gotten more snow than we did back in Ashland. I'm guessing maybe six inches, and it's all fresh. Perfect for sledding and building snowmen!

As we drive down the long lane toward the buildings, the van grows quiet with nothing but a couple dozen wows squirting out of our mouths. The kids sitting near the van windows, including me, have our noses squished against the glass, and the kids in the middle are standing and stretching their necks to look out.

"Sit down, you kids!" Mr. Bill says. "We'll stop soon. Then you can gawk all you want."

The camp, set high in the Pocono Mountains, looks like a scene in the Swiss Alps. I know all about the Swiss Alps because we just studied Switzerland in geography class. As we approach the center of the camp, I spot several large log buildings straight ahead covered in snow and sparkling in the sunshine like diamond dust. Some of the snow on the roofs dance in wisps from the wind, flying in all directions.

The two buildings Captain Ar points out are the registration/dining hall and gymnasium. I'm guessing the pool table is in the gym and wondering if me and Runner will even have any time to shoot a game or two. To the left of the two big buildings, a sloping hill hugs at least a dozen chalets nestled in towering pine trees. The chalets, made with logs and trimmed in red and gold, are all weighed down with massive globs of white. Some of the chalets hiding under the pines are dripping with icicles where the sun's rays have been able to peek through.

"Double wow!" I say as my eyes feast on the site. "This place is so cool."

"Cool?" Leona jokes. "Don't think so. How 'bout frigid?"

"Look over there!" Runner says as we pull in front of one of the main buildings.

"Where?" Coochie says.

"To your right," Runner says. "Look at the kids skating on the pond down there."

"And they're sledding on that big slope over there." Trudy points in the same direction. "Ooh, I can't wait to do that."

"So ... there *are* other kids here." I zero in on the fun about a football field away.

"Yes!" Coochie says. "I wonder when we get to meet them."

"All in good time," Captain Ar says as she parks and turns off the van. "We need to get you all registered and settled in your chalets. Then it'll be time for lunch. After that, your fun may begin."

After Captain Ar registers us, we gals go to chalet number four, and the boys go to chalet number eight.

The chalet is so cool inside, with six sets of bunkbeds and a little side bathroom. On the wall to the right just inside the main door is a cuckoo clock, and as we walk inside the chalet, the clock "coo coos" eleven times, and a cute little red bird pops out from an opened door. The bird is a cardinal. I know it's a cardinal because I learned about different birds in science class.

The whole chalet is made of pretty, shiny wood just like I imagine chalets look in Switzerland. I claim the bottom of one bunk, and Leona takes the top. Trudy throws her overnight bag on the bottom of another bunk while Gail takes the top, and Captain Ar puts her stuff on the bottom of a third set.

DOUBLE TROUBLE AT THE PIONEER TUNNEL

After we unpack and "freshen up," we head to the dining hall and find ourselves in a steady flow with other kids who were also heading for lunch.

Captain Ar had told Runner and me back home that she'd "deeply appreciate" if we'd buddy up with the twins as soon as we arrive at camp. I paired up with Gail as soon as we stepped off the van. Now I'm walking practically arm-in-arm with her, trying to get her to talk a little.

"Have you ever seen such a neat place, Gail?" I ask.

"Nope," she squirts out.

"What would you like to do first?"

"I never ice skated in my life," she grumbles, "and the only sleigh riding I've done is with a big cardboard box." She points to the sledding hill. "I saw kids going down over there in stupid inner tubes. How do you do that?"

"I'm sure you'll catch on to both those things if you try them. And I think there'll be other things to do too. Maybe we'll have a snowman building competition or a snowball fight with some of the other groups. That'll be fun."

"Maybe," she spits out.

"Wow," I whisper to Leona and Trudy walking just inches in front of me. "Look at all the kids here. There must be at least fifty besides us."

"I hope we get to meet some cute guys," Leona says. "I'd like to get to know a dreamboat or two."

"Me too," Trudy says.

"Not me," I whisper to them. "I've already met my dreamboat."

Inside the dining hall, I notice it's all made of pretty wood too. Except for the gray tile floor. I can't help but look up and see the neatest wagon wheel lights, eight of them, hanging on long chains from big wooden beams crisscrossing the ceiling. I also notice to my left a long, busy counter in front of a small kitchen. Three ladies wearing hair nets, bright red "Marching Forward Camp" aprons over pink sweatshirts and black slacks are working like crazy, stirring stuff, pouring stuff, and putting large trays of food in a certain order.

Mr. Bill makes a beeline to a roly-poly man who, even though he's wearing a black cowboy hat, a red checkered shirt, blue jeans, and a big fancy belt with a shiny buckle, could pass for Santa's twin.

In seconds, Mr. Bill joins us, says something to Captain Ar, and she directs us to a cluster of cafeteria tables in the far-right corner near the restrooms. She and Trudy sit across from me, Gail, and Leona. The boys and Mr. Bill sit to our right at another table. Runner's sitting with Mr. Bill on the opposite side of our tables, and that makes it real easy for me to keep an eye on Runner.

As all the other kids and their leaders find their designated places, my gaze sweeps the large room, and I spot some really awesome-looking boys. But none can measure up to Runner. I also spot two girls goo-goo eyeing him from the table next to our boys. I can feel my face heat up bigtime, and I have to look away before I storm right over to those girls and tell them to get their stupid eyes off my dreamboat.

I take a deep breath as my attention shifts to Captain Ar, who's staring at me with those all-knowing blue eyes and her arms crossed. She knows me like the back of her hand, and I immediately shoot straight up in my chair and give her a Cheshire cat grin.

The whole place smells delicious, although I can't zero in on what the smell is exactly. I count the different groups that are here, six counting us, and notice we're all filling up about two-thirds of the tables, so I'm guessing this place could hold about a hundred or so kids at one time.

While we gab and eye all the kids with nerve-jerking scrutiny, Santa steps up on a small platform near the serving counter and grabs a floor mike.

DOUBLE TROUBLE AT THE PIONEER TUNNEL

"Attention, ladies and gentlemen."

The microphone squeals so loud we have to cover our ears, so the man yanks it away from his mouth. Drawing it back slowly, he says, "Sorry about that, folks. Anyway, I'm Mr. Thoroway, the camp director, and I'd like to welcome each and every one of you here. For those of you who just arrived, I'm sure your team leaders have reviewed our rules, which aren't many, so you know how to conduct yourselves accordingly. I'm sure you're all anxious to get back out in the snow, get soaking wet, and make new friends. We have a freezing, fun-packed schedule for you until two o'clock tomorrow, so get ready. I hope you all brought your long johns."

A round of cheers and applause breaks out, and we join in.

"I'm also sure you're all ready for lunch. Today we have barbecue, chips, lemonade, chocolate chip cookies, and cocoa."

"Anything's better than hot dogs!" Moose yells out, and everybody laughs, even the twins.

"Moose!" Mr. Bill puts his finger to his lips. "Sh-h-h."

"Oops," Moose says, and we all laugh again.

"Har dee har har." Gail throws out a mocking laugh, and I poke my elbow in her side.

"Knock it off," I whisper.

Captain Ar scowls in our direction as she subtly shakes her head. I'm not sure if she's doing that for Gail's or my benefit. Whatever. I shoot straight up in my chair again and whisper, "Sorry."

Mr. Thoroway gets our attention with his squealing mike. "Okay, gang. Here's what we have planned for you over the next day or so. After lunch, we'll have each team build their own forts and have a snowball battle on the open field behind this building. Then we'll have snow shovel and cardboard box races down the sledding hill, so pick your fastest down-hill-on-snow people." The man chuckles at his last words while the rest of us just stare.

"I can do that," Gail whispers. "I'm really good with cardboard."

"We'll see," I whisper back.

Captain Ar puts her finger to her lips. "Girls, sh-h-h."

"After supper," Mr. Thoroway continues, "we'll have ice skating and regular sledding or tubing. You who just arrived might not know that our pond and slopes are well lit, and if the sky is clear with a full moon as the weatherman predicted, the whole place will look like an electric Christmas yard. You'll be able to do those activities until nine o'clock tonight."

Everybody claps and cheers again with smiles filling the entire room.

"Youth for Truth group from Elmira, New York, where are you?" Mr. Thoroway asks.

A group just to our right hoot, and about twenty kids holler, "Here!"

Mr. Thoroway holds up a paper. "I see here you're the team to beat in snow fort building. You won last evening's competition by beating the other three groups. Congratulations! Your prize is one that probably won't last too long, but I'm sure you'll enjoy it. You each can get a free ice cream cone at our snack bar. Let's give them a hand."

Everyone claps while the winners smile, a few boys poking up their thumbs.

"Where's the group from the Salvation Army Post in Ashland, Pennsylvania?" Mr. Thoroway asks.

We all raise our hands and yell, "Back here!"

"I welcome you all," he says, "and I trust you'll have a wonderful time and make a lot of new friends."

Captain Ar nods and her lips gesture, "Thank you."

Mr. Thoroway glances at his kitchen staff. "I think our lunch is ready."

DOUBLE TROUBLE AT THE PIONEER TUNNEL

One lady holding up a serving spoon nods her head yes.

"All right," Mr. Thoroway says. "Let's pray, and we'll have you line up according to the number on the card in the center of your tables.

I look at the card that has "ONE" printed on it. "We're first!"

"Aw right!" I hear Moose say. "We're number two!"

"I think that's Mr. Thoroway's special way of welcoming our group here," Captain Ar says as she stands. "Now quiet down while the man prays. Then we'll stampede the food line!"

It's about two o'clock in the afternoon, I'm walking toward sledding slope number one after a quick visit to the restroom, and I hear Captain Ar yell, "Pockets, watch out!"

I spin around and focus on her waving and rushing toward me from the registration office, but in seconds I'm swept off my feet, flip upside down, and land flat on my face in the snow. I shake my head to get a grip and stagger to stand. I spot Gail and Dale in a huge black inner tube charging down the hill a stone's throw away from me. I feel the hair on the back of my neck prickle, and although the rest of me is as cold as an icicle, my face heats up bigtime. The hateful side of me kicks in, and I'm just about ready to scream, "You brats!" But then—

"Honey, are you all right?" Captain Ar hurries to my side and wipes snow off my face.

I work on dusting off the snow from all my clothes. "Yeah, I'm okay, but what are those two doing over here on slope two? We're all supposed to be on slope one."

"I have a feeling those two kids lost their patience waiting for a turn to go down the hill. And I have a feeling they snuck away from the group without Bill noticing while I had business in the office. Now we have a problem. You head back to the group. I'll take care of the twins."

And I know exactly what that means.

It's eleven o'clock at night, and after the day of sledding, ice skating, snowman building, a chicken finger supper, a devotion time with Mr. Thoroway, table games, and a few games of pool with Runner, then sledding again until nine o'clock, my whole body melts into the soft mattress. My eyes close, and as I drift away, I take a deep breath and think about the twins and how they spent the rest of the afternoon sitting and fuming beside Captain Ar and Mr. Bill, watching the rest of us having fun and winning the snowman building contest! I also think back to the really cool devotion time Captain Ar had with us girls just a little while ago here in the chalet, sitting in a tight circle on the floor with our blankets wrapped around us.

"Girls," she said, "when we pulled into the camp earlier today, what impressed you the most when you saw the place?"

Leona popped her hand in the air. "Ooh, I love the buildings. They're all so pretty, especially these chalets with their gold and red trim."

Trudy put up her hand. "And I like the way the sledding hill and pond look. You just wanna be there."

"Anything else?" Captain Ar said.

I looked at Gail, and she was hanging on a super pout as she stared at the floor with her arms folded and legs crossed, not moving one teensy, weensy muscle. I could tell she was ticked to the high heavens about losing all her playtime earlier. No way was she gonna say anything. *When is that kid gonna learn what Captain Ar says, she means?*

DOUBLE TROUBLE AT THE PIONEER TUNNEL

I glanced back at Captain Ar and raised my hand.

"Yes, Pockets?"

"Well, the first thing about this place that got my attention was how the fresh snow looked so amazing. It was so clean and white and sparkly, it almost hurt my eyes to look at it. It's one of the neatest things I've ever seen."

"You're right," Captain Ar said. "Now, I want to share a Bible verse about snow with all of you."

"There's a Bible verse about snow?" Trudy asked.

"Yes," Captain Ar said. "There are quite a few verses about snow in the Bible. This one is in the book of Psalms, chapter fifty-one. That psalm is so beautiful, just like the snow. The psalm starts with this verse: 'Have mercy upon me, O God, according to thy lovingkindness: according unto the multitude of thy tender mercies blot out my transgressions.' Do any of you know what the word transgression means?"

"It means sin," I said. "Stuff we do that doesn't please God."

"That's right," Captain Ar said. "This psalm talks about our sins and how we should ask the Lord to forgive us."

"But how does snow fit in to all this?" Trudy asked.

Captain Ar gave us her best smile. "Trudy, I'm so glad you asked. Verses seven to ten in this beautiful psalm tell us what we can do to have God forgive us. 'Purge me with hyssop, and I shall be clean. Wash me, and I shall be whiter than snow. Make me to hear joy and gladness that the bones which thou hast broken may rejoice. Hide thy face from my sins and blot out all mine iniquities. Create in me a clean heart, O God; and renew a right spirit within me.'"

Trudy scrunched up her face. "But I'm still not getting how snow fits in with all that."

"You see, girls, the psalmist compares the brilliance of clean snow to our clean hearts when we ask God to forgive us of all our sins. When you accept Jesus as your Savior, you then have a right spirit, the Holy Spirit, inside of you, and you don't want to keep doing bad things like lying or disobeying. But when we do mess up and ask God to forgive us, he does right away."

"Oh, I get it," Leona said. "I asked Jesus to save me, and I do think real different now."

"Me too," Trudy said.

"Me too," I said. "And what does hyssop mean?" I looked at Gail still trying to stare a hole through the floor.

"I'm glad you asked about hyssop," Captain Ar said. "I looked up that word. It's a plant, some kind of mint from Europe. It has aromatic and pungent leaves used in perfume and as a seasoning in food. And … it's often used as a remedy for bruises. That is so very interesting. Purging, or removing, with hyssop means your bruises, or sins, are washed away, and besides being as white as snow, you will also smell *delicious*!"

We all laughed.

Except Gail.

While lying in bed and thinking about earlier in the evening, I hear Leona above me snoring up a storm. My sleepy brain brings me back from mint plants in Europe that Captain Ar had told us about to right now and then to the border of Dreamland. I take another long, deep breath and am almost gone. But I hear a strange sound that alerts my senses. The door of the chalet inches open and inches shut seconds later.

I slowly lift my head and look across the room at the other bunks, the full moon lighting the room just enough to see. Captain Ar is sound asleep, and Trudy's snoring away but …

Gail is gone.

Now I'm more than wide awake, lying here wondering what to do. I look at Captain Ar and think I should wake

DOUBLE TROUBLE AT THE PIONEER TUNNEL

her up. But she looked so tired earlier tonight, I figure I can do something and not bother her. I can fix this myself.

I decide to go after the little Pawson sneak and get her back in her bunk before anyone knows. I assume she might be just on the other side of the door. *I wonder what she's up to.*

In about a minute flat and not making one iota of a sound, I get dressed—boots, coat, hood, gloves, and all—and inch my way outside.

With the help of the silvery moon and the glowing streetlights all over the place, I look toward the sledding slope. I can't believe what I'm seeing. How did that little monster get over there so fast? Gail and her brother are speeding down the hill on a gigantic inner tube!

My gaze sweeps the whole scene, and nothing else is moving. Nothing. There's not even a hint of a breeze, and everything is dead silent. Everything looks like a Currier and Ives Christmas card. Except Gail and Dale. They look like a "Champion Rule Breakers" card.

I run as fast as my boots can take me to the twins, who are just coming in for a landing at the bottom of the hill. Spinning in the inner tube as it slows down then stops on the smooth snow, they don't see me coming.

"Boy," I say in the loudest whisper I can muster as I run up to them. "Are you two ever in big trouble now!"

They jump off the inner tube like they were sitting on hot coals, and their eyes almost pop out of their hooded heads as they stare at me.

"What are you doing here?" Gail says. "Get lost."

I grab the inner tube. "Get back to your bunks now, and I won't say anything."

"Yeah, right." Dale grabs the inner tube and tries to take it away from me.

"Give us that!" Gail grabs the inner tube, and they team up against me, pulling with all their might.

"Let it go, you brats!" I say as I pull my guts out.

We tumble to the ground and wrestle with the inner tube as the twins try their best to get it from me.

"You scuzz bag!" Gail yells. "Let go!"

"All right. That's enough!" I hear an all-too-familiar voice say.

The three of us let go of the inner tube like it's those hot coals and scramble to our feet.

There stands Captain Ar, with the angriest face I've ever seen on her.

"Aw rats," Dale says.

Forget the brat twins.

I think I'm sunk.

CHAPTER TEN

"You three, back to your bunks right now," Captain Ar orders.

Gail sticks her tongue out at me as we start walking.

I've never wanted to smack anyone as much as I'd like to smack her.

As we head toward the chalets, Mr. Bill comes charging toward us.

"What's going on?" he says. "I just noticed that someone was not in his bunk." He gives Dale a disgusted look.

Dale hangs on a "Who cares?" face.

"Oh," Captain Ar says, "these three decided to go tubing when they'd have the slopes all to themselves."

Gail points at me and squeals, "It was her idea!"

"Yeah!" Dale says. "She said she'd meet us out here as soon as everybody was asleep."

"But I—"

Captain Ar raises her palm toward me. "Not now, Pockets. We'll discuss this all in the morning first thing after breakfast." She turns toward Dale. "Young man, you go with Mr. Bill right this minute, and don't get any more bright ideas about having fun all by yourself."

I learned a long time ago that when Captain Ar gives me orders, I should keep my big, fat mouth shut and just obey. Forget trying to argue with her or change her mind.

DOUBLE TROUBLE AT THE PIONEER TUNNEL

So, as we all head back to our chalets, no one blabs a word. I can tell Captain Ar is not only angry with us, but she's totally disappointed in me, thinking I was a part of this fiasco.

I can't wait to tell her what really happened. Maybe she'll have mercy on me. On the other hand, I was stupid. Stupid! What was I thinking? Sometimes I think because I've been in counseling with Captain Ar almost the longest of any of the other kids that I can be the big shot and take things into my own hands. Stupid. That's all I am. *Stupid, stupid, stupid.*

And I never gave praying for God's help a second thought. Stupid.

The next morning after packing all our overnight bags in the Volkswagen and having breakfast—I hardly ate a crumb—me, the brats, Captain Ar, and Mr. Bill are sitting at our table number one. The rest of the dining room is echo empty except for the kitchen ladies banging pots and pans and putting food away in the kitchen.

All the rest of the kids left five minutes ago.

As Runner walked past and eyed me plastered to my seat, he gave me the sweetest look of concern and raised his palms.

Stone-faced, I just shook my head.

Everybody's out there building forts and getting ready for a snowball battle, something I was dying to do since we came yesterday. But here I sit. In big trouble. All my own doing. Miss Know-It-All-Big-Shot.

"Pockets," Captain Ar says to me. "Please go and sit at table twenty over there." She points to the one nearest the entrance on the other end of the room. "Mr. Bill and I have some things to discuss with Gail and Dale."

"Yes, ma'am," I say and hightail it to the table. I station myself so I can watch every move the four of them make. Even though I know Captain Ar is steaming, I also know the woman has amazing self-control. Something I need to learn. And Mr. Bill? He's usually the picture of patience, although right now I can see he doesn't have even an inkling of it by the look on his face.

The twins are slumped in their chairs with their arms folded, but I know Captain Ar is insisting that they sit up straight and look at her and Mr. Bill, or they'll be there all morning until the kids obey.

In a minute or two, Gail and Dale finally shape up, and a few minutes later, Mr. Bill and the twins leave, a stern face on the man and red-faced anger oozing out of the two. But as they hurry by, I notice tears flooding the kids' eyes. Wow! Captain Ar must have hammered them good.

"Pockets, come here now!" Captain Ar gestures for me to join her.

As I sit across from her, my heart starts racing like I just ran all the way up *and* down the sledding slopes. I stare into the woman's all-knowing, piercing blue eyes, and my own pleading blue eyes fill with tears.

"I'm sorry," I say, "but it wasn't my idea to go on the slopes last night. I didn't know anything about it. But I saw Gail wasn't in her bunk, so I went after her to bring her back before anyone saw her. I didn't want to disturb you because I knew you were so tired. You know I wouldn't disobey you."

"Pockets, Pockets, Pockets, when will you ever learn?" She shakes her head and forces out a smile. "It wasn't too long ago I told you to come to me or Mr. Bill when trouble's brewing, especially with the twins. They're experts at causing trouble. You should know that by now."

"You would think," I say with a sigh. I cross my arms so she can't see how my hands are shaking.

DOUBLE TROUBLE AT THE PIONEER TUNNEL

"So, would you agree that you *did* disobey?"

"Y-Yes, ma'am."

"And you should know that I care about you—however, you should also know when I say something, I mean it."

I wipe a tear from each eye. "Yes, I do know that."

"Honey, you'll be spending the morning by my side. Gail will be on my other side. You'll be able to participate in the activities after lunch until we leave at two. But the twins' fun is over as far as activities here at the camp."

Now my floodgates burst open, and the tears stream down my face. "But I wasn't part of their scheme. I'm not lying!"

"I know you're telling me the truth." Captain Ar's eyes water. "I'm not grounding you because of that. I could list two or three infractions you committed, but let's just say you disobeyed. Pockets, you should have come to me and let me handle the situation."

"I know, I know." I lower my head and wipe the tears.

As far as me spending time with Captain Ar, that's a no-brainer. I love every minute I spend with her. I love and respect her so much, I'd even jump off a cliff or eat Brussels sprouts if she asked me. But this? I'll be embarrassed to the high hilt when all the kids see me glued to her side. I'll never live it down. My brain is churning different plots. I want to ask her to let me serve time back at the post, like no pool table for a month, which would kill me. But then I get my senses back. I know better than to try to change the woman's mind.

"Let me pray with you," Captain Ar says as she folds her hands on the table. "I really hope you've learned a good lesson through this."

"I have." I sniffle. "I have."

At two o'clock sharp, we say goodbye to the camp and a few friends we made. Several of us exchange addresses and phone numbers. Sally, a cool kid from New York and my new friend, is the only one who asks me why I didn't do anything all morning. All I tell her is I had "issues."

Nobody from our post, except Runner, asks me what happened. They all know I broke some rule. Runner just wanted to know because he cares. Then there's Moose. He doesn't say anything, but his look tells me what he's thinking—*Ha ha. You got caught.* He's such an immature snob.

On our way to Honesdale and Miss McGinnis, the van buzzes with exciting stories and laughter. My best friend, cheerleader Leona, sweeps her wavy hair off her brow more than once as she fills me in on the two "absolutely dreamy" boys she met. Everybody's mouths are in high gear.

Except the twins.

Except me.

I'm still in shock at how stupid I was to get grounded. The worst part of all was how I disappointed Captain Ar. As I slump in the van seat, I make up my mind to never, ever do anything that ridiculous again. No sir-ee. From now on, I go to her, especially if it involves the two obnoxious terrors. And I certainly need to pray for at least a ton of patience if Captain Ar expects me to work with the girl tornado anymore.

In a half hour, we pull into the Hot Shot Poolroom in Honesdale. Miss McGinnis greets us in her cool billiard ball outfit as we all rush inside like a bunch of ducks heading for the pond. The poolroom opens for business only at five o'clock, so the place is empty except for us.

Me, Captain Ar, and Runner are all carrying our cue sticks in their cases, ready for a few hours of pure pool bliss.

DOUBLE TROUBLE AT THE PIONEER TUNNEL

Those of us who had been here before smile to beat the band when Miss McGinnis shakes all our hands. Moose, Gail, and Dale just freeze on their spots with their mouths hanging open as they gawk at the place. I think the three of them are thinking nice thoughts for a change, although Gail's probably ready to spit nails because her hateful behavior at the camp caused her to lose her game with the Billiard Queen.

Even though I've been here before, I can't help letting my eyes feast on this amazing place. Besides the eight pool tables with shiny balls, green cloths, and lights with bright colored glass shades, there are fancy wood racks for the cue sticks mounted on the walls, a rack for each table. Dark blue folding chairs are scattered along the walls. There aren't many chairs, maybe two or three per table. Why should there be more chairs when people are coming here to shoot pool, not sit?

The walls are a real pale pinkish orange, kind of the color of a ripe peach, and the carpet is dark green with a pattern that looks like grass. In between the cue racks on the walls are framed pictures of billiard heroes—Willie Mosconi, Minnesota Fats, Luther Lassiter, U.J. Puckett, Cowboy Jimmy Moore, many of the big shots in the pool world ... and ... yes! A picture of Ruth is there too.

I take a quick glance at the other kids, and their eyes are all still bugging out.

"Kids," Miss McGinnis says, "remember that the restrooms are in the back corner, and we have donuts and hot chocolate for you at our snack counter." She points, and we all look to the back of the large room. Nick, the same man we met the last time, is working behind the counter. Miss McGinnis had told us he's the owner of the place. He looks at us and waves. He's chubby and probably a little older than Captain Ar. And he's ancient, like maybe forty. He's bald, and he's wearing a navy blue janitor-type suit.

Miss McGinnis adds, "After your snack, we'll pair everyone for the pool games. And I'll need to see Moose, Trudy, and Gail right away."

I'm sure Captain Ar called Miss McGinnis about Gail. I wonder who'll get to shoot with Miss McGinnis now for that third game.

We all line up for our snack then huddle around card tables near the counter. It doesn't take a bunch of kids long to scarf down a couple dozen donuts and gigantic cups of hot chocolate. As we finish, Miss McGinnis joins us and gets our attention.

"Kids, I'm going to assign each of you in pairs to a pool table where you may play as many games as you like while I shoot with your three winners. I'm going to start with Gail, so counting the two winners waiting to shoot with me, there are ten of you. The pairs are Moose and Reuben, Coochie and Dale, Trudy and Leona, and I've paired up Runner with Bill and Pockets with Captain Masters. So, Gail, you may come with me, and we'll go to table eight."

If I had had a wad of gum in my mouth, I would've swallowed it. Miss Twelve-and-a-half-years-old Birthday Girl gets to shoot? After all that kid's done the last twenty-four hours? And Dale gets to shoot too? I'm in total shock. How could Captain Ar allow this?

CHAPTER ELEVEN

Oh, if I could get my hands on those two, they'd be wrapped in cellophane and stuck in a corner. My mouth drops open at what I just heard as Captain Ar comes to my side. "Get your cue stick, Pockets. How about some nine ball?"

"Sure," I say without even a hint of a stingy smile and grab my cue from its case and screw the two parts of the stick together.

All over the room, the smacking of pool balls echoes with exciting chatter. Right now, shooting pool is the farthest thing from my confused, angry mind.

Captain Ar looks at me with concern dripping all over her face. "Pockets, what's wrong? Are you not feeling well?"

"N-No, I'm fine."

She walks right up to me and gently touches my shoulder. "I know you better than that. There's something wrong."

For the first time since I met the woman, I'm mad as a caged cougar at her. I take a deep breath and try to calm down. "H-How could you let Gail shoot pool with Miss McGinnis after all that kid's done on our trip?"

"Oh, so that's it." Captain Ar looks at me as if she knew all along what's wrong with me. I think she knows me better than I know me. She leans her stick against the wall and grabs my hand. "Please come with me."

I lean my cue against the wall, and we walk to the back of the room. She gestures for me to sit at one of the card tables. She sits across from me and waits until I calm down. I hate when she does that. I take a few deep breaths while my stare locks on hers. I fold my arms and get ready for a good explanation ... as if she would even owe me one.

We sit in silence for what seems like at least three hours. It was three minutes.

Then Captain Ar asks me, "Pockets, I want to ask you a question."

I just nod.

"Did Gail break any rules here?"

I pause then say, "Well, no. But look at—"

She raises her palm toward me. "Young lady, I don't feel that I owe anyone an explanation for what Bill and I decided concerning the twins. You'll have to just trust my judgment on things like this. Until you're old enough to run your *own* life and then maybe some others, you need to just accept the decisions grown-ups make concerning you and no one else."

I just stare at her.

"While Gail spent the day with me, she actually told me she was sorry, and I believed her."

"She was probably lying to get on your good side."

"I don't think so. I think she was sincere. Pockets, don't you have the same battle between doing right and wrong as these twins have?"

"Well, yes, but I ask God to forgive me, and he does."

"Honey, do you know what that's called?"

"No, what?"

"That's called God's grace. He forgives all we've ever done when we ask him just because he loves us so much. I want Gail to know we love her. But more than that, I want her to experience God's love and know what God's grace means. My allowing her to shoot pool was an act of grace. I could just as easily have told her she couldn't shoot pool because of her behavior. But I explained to her in detail why I was allowing her to shoot with Miss McGinnis. When I finished, Gail actually said thank you."

I just sit and stare at the table and think through everything the woman is saying.

"Pockets."

I finally look at her.

"I think you keep forgetting you were once where Gail is. She's a lonely, scared kid who is love starved. I'm praying we can love her through her problems so she can know the love of God and be a happy kid. Her brother too."

I stare at those blue eyes that can almost read my every thought.

"And ... how about you, Pockets?"

I just shrug.

"You haven't been happy lately, have you?"

"Well, yes—except when it comes to the twins."

"Do you know what you're doing to yourself?"

I just shake my head.

"You're letting circumstances, and in this case other kids, take your joy from you. I can only guess you've not spent a lot of time asking God to help you love the twins, have you?"

"No, ma'am." I shake my head again.

Captain Ar gives me her best smile. "All you need to do is ask him. He'll also give you the wisdom you need to deal with Gail. In the book of James chapter one, part of verse five says, 'If any of you lack wisdom, let him ask of God, that giveth to all men liberally.' You just try asking God for love and wisdom, and you'll be very surprised what happens, not only with you, but with Gail."

"I'll try," I say and force a smile back.

DOUBLE TROUBLE AT THE PIONEER TUNNEL

"Good girl. Now, I have an apology to make."

I just look at those piercing blue eyes.

"Pockets, I am very sorry for jumping to the conclusion that you were involved with the twins and their nighttime sledding scheme. I know you better than that, and I'm sorry I didn't handle your situation better. To be fair, I had to discipline you, but on second thought, I might have done something differently." Her eyes water with tears. "Will you forgive me?"

Wow. The woman really is sorry. "Of course, I forgive you. You had to do what you had to do."

"But not in that way. I care about you very much, and I was, well, let's just say, it could have been handled much better."

"I understand. You're human, just like the rest of us." *But she's still my hero.*

"Oh, how right you are." She stands and squeezes my shoulder. "Now, let's go have some fun."

We shoot pool and have a ball—get the pun?—until about five o'clock. Miss McGinnis has all us kids rotate to different tables so we have a chance to shoot with one another and Captain Ar. Mr. Bill hangs out with Nick at the food counter. Mr. Bill does love his coffee.

The whole time I'm shooting with Captain Ar, I keep my eye on Gail, watching how she acts. My mouth drops open more than once when I notice how good she picks up the game as Miss McGinnis gives her pointers. Gail takes to the rack of balls like a mother hen takes to her nest of eggs. And Gail actually smiles bigtime often and looks at the Billiard Queen in a whole new admiring light. Maybe there is hope for that kid after all!

I shift my spying eye to Dale as he tries to shoot, and … well, that's another story. I must have heard him spout "Aw rats!" at least a dozen times. He's probably better at smashing things with a baseball bat.

After we scarf down a farewell snack of hot dogs, chips, and root beer soda, Miss McGinnis gives us a final send-off, and we head home.

By the time we pull in at the post around eight o'clock, the wild chatter in the van has vanished, and some kids, including Leona, are even snoring up a storm. But up front, Gail is gabbing and rambling on like her mouth is stuck in high gear. Could this be the start of seeing a new Gail?

"... And I got in big trouble, but it wasn't my fault. It was the twins' fault, and then they got me grounded, but when we got to the poolroom in Honesdale—"

"Whoa, Tommi Jo!" Meemaw says. "One thing at a time." She sips her coffee as we sit at the kitchen table. Pop too! For him to be here with us on a Saturday night at nine o'clock is a real rare event. He's munching chips, smoking a cigar, and drinking a bottle of beer, trying real hard to seem interested in what I'm saying. But if I know my pop, in a few minutes, he'll head off to Joe's to shoot pool until the wee hours. He craves billiards at Joe's like I used to. At least, he's not hanging out at the bar anymore, and that's a real good thing.

"Did you get to shoot pool with that McGinnis lady?" he asks, showing his first spark of interest in the whole conversation.

"Pop," I say, "you should see her shoot. She even did some trick shots. One time she jumped the cue ball over three other balls to make a corner shot. She also set all fifteen balls near each pocket in such a combination that she made all the balls with one shot. She's amazing."

"I'd love to see her shoot sometime," he says then sips his bottle.

DOUBLE TROUBLE AT THE PIONEER TUNNEL

"If she ever stops by at the post again, I'll sure let you know," I say.

Meemaw rests her chin on her closed fist. My sweet grandma looks dog tired, as usual, from that factory job. But ever since she turned her life over to God, she has a sparkle in her eyes, especially when she smiles. Captain Ar says that glow is the joy of Jesus coming out from a new, clean heart.

"So, Tommi Jo," Meemaw asks, "what part of the snow camp did you like the best?"

"Hm-m-m." I think for a long minute. I've been so focused on the twins and their antics, I haven't really thought about the good stuff. "Well, let's see. Oh! Runner and I got to shoot pool on their little pool table. It wasn't as nice as the one at Joe's or at our post, but it was still fun. And tubing down the camp's really steep slopes was a blast. There were a lot of other kids there, even some from New York. I made a new friend named Sally. We're gonna write to each other. And yesterday after supper, we all met in the gymnasium, and Mr. Thoroway talked to us about Jesus and forgiving people who hurt us. That was pretty good."

Meemaw giggles. "I knew you'd say something about Runner."

My cheeks fire up, and I rush to the refrigerator to grab a bottle of Coke. "He's just a friend. That's all." I pry the lid off and take a swig.

"I sure miss him at Joe's," Pop says. "Nobody could beat us. Why'd he ever stop coming there anyway?"

I walk back to my chair. "Pop, since he gave his life to Jesus, he doesn't feel that's the place for him anymore."

"That's too much religion," he says. "It takes all the fun out of life."

"Pop," I say, "I have lots of fun since I became a Christian. And I've made a lot of new friends, good friends, who don't let me down."

Meemaw finishes her coffee. "Tom, life's not fun and games all the time. We can find happiness other ways."

"Like how?" Pop says sharply.

"Like helping others," Meemaw says. "There's great joy in making other folks happy. Why just the other day, Pastor Sutcliff and his wife, Evanne, went to visit the Pawsons. Parnell wasn't there, but Evanne told me they had a wonderful talk with Hattie. She couldn't thank them enough for all the food and help we've been sending in. Because of that, Evanne is going to start a Bible study with Hattie, and Pastor will have one with Parnell if—"

"Parnell, hmmph," Pop growls. "If anybody needs religion, it's him."

I get ready to say something but clamp my big, fat mouth shut and take a gulp of soda.

Meemaw takes her cup to the sink and rinses it. "Our pastor will have a Bible study with you too, Tom, if you want."

"Nah, not right now," he says and finishes his bottle of beer.

Meemaw comes back to the table, wipes it clean with a dishcloth, and sits with us again. "I found out something really interesting when I took that pot of spaghetti to Hattie last Tuesday."

"What's that, Meemaw?"

"Hattie is quite the delightful person, even though she's in a lot of pain most of the time."

"What's wrong with her?" I ask.

"It's probably that miserable husband of hers," Pop says.

"They really don't know," Meemaw says. "She has a lot of swelling in her legs, and the more she's on her feet, the more they swell, sometimes so bad she can't even get her shoes on. The doctor thinks it might be extreme arthritis or something like that, but they just don't know.

DOUBLE TROUBLE AT THE PIONEER TUNNEL

She's been like that for the last eight years, ever since she turned her ankle playing with the twins in the backyard. She tripped over a baseball bat and almost broke her foot. Ever since then, she's been going to doctors, even specialists in Philly, but no one has an answer. I really pity her and the kids. We ladies in the church are going to make it a routine for us to take in meals a few times a week and even clean their house once a month. She's bedridden most of the time and can't do much of anything. The place is a mess. By the way, Tommi Jo, next Saturday morning I'm scheduled to take a pot of chili to them and tidy up the place for an hour or so. I want to know if you'd like to go with me and meet Hattie. It might give you a whole new perspective on why the twins are the way they are. We'll be home in plenty of time for you to have lunch and get to the bowling alley for your four-hour shift."

"I guess I can," I say with hardly an ounce of enthusiasm.

Pop spurts out, "If that no-good husband of hers would get his act together, things wouldn't be so bad with them."

"Well," Meemaw says, "if we show that family the love of Christ, we have no idea what could happen. Parnell could—"

"Get religion?" Pop says. "That would be a miracle."

"Pop," I say, "God does a lot of miracles."

"Yes, Tom," Meemaw says. "Prayer can change things. You'll see."

"Hmmph," is all Pop offers.

"Tommi Jo," Meemaw says as she stands, "now that Runner's parents are bringing the twins to church every Sunday, Pastor Sutcliff would like different families to invite the kids to dinner after church then take them home sometime in the afternoon. I told him we can start the ball rolling by having them here tomorrow, that is, Tom, if you can drive them home afterward. Will you be here for dinner?"

"As long as Parnell's not with them, I'll get them home," Pop says and pushes away from the table. "I'll just cut my pool time a little short tonight, so I'm up in time for the noon meal tomorrow."

"Thank you," Meemaw says. "Tommi Jo, I made your favorite dish for dinner tomorrow. Blind pigeons. So, I want you to be on your best behavior."

I almost choke on my last mouthful of soda as I listen to this last conversation. "You've got to be kidding! The twins are coming here? No way."

CHAPTER TWELVE

"I'm twelve-and-a-half," Gail spurts out at our kitchen table.

I can't stand it! I just can't stand it! What a twerp!

Gail's sitting between Dale and Pop while me and Meemaw get the dinner ready.

While I pour lemonade in three glasses at the table, I'm sizzling inside, ready to explode. Then I remember Captain Ar reminding me to pray about these two br—I mean kids—and my rotten attitude.

"So, you two are almost thirteen. I see," Meemaw says as she preps the meal in the slow cooker on the stove and glances at Gail. "When's your birthday then?"

"June 28," Dale practically yells.

Meemaw unplugs the slow cooker, and at the table she places the cooker next to a big bowl of mashed potatoes.

I study the look on her face and know she's figuring that June is only four months away, not six months.

"Why, that's when Tommi Jo's birthday is," Pop throws in. "What a coincidence."

"Whose Tommi Jo?" Gail asks.

I point my thumb at my chest. "That's me. It's my real name."

"Oh," Gail says.

"Well," Meemaw says, "we must have a party when June rolls around."

DOUBLE TROUBLE AT THE PIONEER TUNNEL

"We ain't never had a birthday party." Dale breaks out in the biggest smile I've ever seen on his freckled face.

I can't imagine having even one ounce of fun at a party with these two. What's Meemaw thinking? But, since this is the first time I've ever really, really noticed Dale smile, I see how bad his teeth are and figure he, probably Gail too, have never been to a dentist.

"Turning thirteen's a big deal," Pop says with a big yawn. His hair hasn't been combed, and he hasn't shaved yet. He has the same work clothes on that he wore yesterday. I'm thinking it's a miracle he's sitting here and not in bed. Last night I heard him come in real late.

I put the lemonade in the fridge, grab the coffee pot, and fill Meemaw's and Pop's cups at the table. I put the coffee pot back on the counter and sit next to Pop. Meemaw grabs her stirring spoon from the top of the stove and finally is able to sit next to me.

I stare at the twins and notice how nice they look. Really nice. I know the church ladies had bought the kids some new clothes, and today the twins are showing off some of the nicest.

First of all, Gail's pigtails are sparkling clean and look like they might have been done just this morning. Maybe her mother felt well enough to braid the pigtails because they look better than I've seen them in weeks. Gail's wearing a really cute outfit—a blue and yellow striped long-sleeved pullover sweater and a navy blue, pleated skirt. Of course, with snow still covering the ground in Ashland, she has her new boots on too. Dale has on a burgundy pullover sweater and dark green trousers with his boots. Although the wind mussed up his shiny hair a little, I can tell it had been parted with a wet comb to flatten the cowlicks before he left home.

"You two look so nice today," Meemaw says to the twins.

"Mommy felt good enough to get out of bed and help us get ready," Gail says.

"Yeah," Dale says. "That doesn't happen often, because she's sick all the time."

I survey our table that looks like it's ready for President Eisenhower. I haven't a clue why Meemaw did what she did, but she got out her best china and silverware. For the Pawson twins! The last time we ate from these blue willow plates on the gorgeous white lace tablecloth was about a year ago when Pastor and Mrs. Sutcliff came after we first started going to church. These dishes and tablecloth are Meemaw's prized treasures passed down from her grandmother. What's Meemaw thinking?

"Now, Tommi Jo," Meemaw says, "will you please pray before we eat?"

"Yes," I say and feel like the biggest hypocrite in Schuylkill County. Why'd she pick on me? She knows how I feel about these twins.

"We always pray before we eat and thank God for the food, don't we, Tommi Jo?" she adds.

"Yes," I say, then I thank God for the food. Short and sweet. Well, let's just say "short."

Meemaw starts spooning out the food from the cooker. "Kids, have you ever had blind pigeons?" She places a large spoonful of the concoction drenched in spaghetti sauce on each of their plates. Then she gives them each a spoonful of mashed potatoes.

Without even a hint of a smile, the twins stare at their plates, at a sauce-soaked "lump" of food about the size of a small hot dog in its bun. But it's no hot dog.

"Where'd you get the pigeons?" Dale tries hard not to make a sour face.

I hear him say "aw rats" under his breath, and I almost burst out laughing.

"Yeah," Gail adds with a look of disgust. "I ain't never ate a pigeon before."

DOUBLE TROUBLE AT THE PIONEER TUNNEL

Again, I have to bite my lip to keep from laughing out loud. I know these two are probably half-starved. Who knows if they had anything to eat at home at all this morning? But they're not at all sure about what's on their plates.

"Kids," Pop says with a chuckle, "they're not really pigeons."

While Meemaw spoons out the dish to the rest of us, she says, "Blind pigeons is just a funny name for a recipe we've handed down through our family. It's made with ground beef, kind of like mini meatloaves wrapped in cabbage leaves, then simmered for a few hours in spaghetti sauce."

"Right," I add with a twinge of sarcasm. "We don't eat pigeons here. It's just a name."

"Go on, kids," Pop says. "Try it. I think you'll like it a lot."

While the rest of us dig in, the twins take their first forkful like the food is deadly poison. Then in a few seconds ...

"Hey," Gail says with a smile, "this is pretty good. I don't taste pigeon at all!"

Dale swallows and stuffs his mouth with another forkful. "Good," he mumbles. "Good."

"And when you're ready for dessert," Meemaw says, "we have brownies topped with vanilla ice cream."

"M-mm," Gail says, shoving more food in her mouth. "I love that."

"Me too," Dale mumbles, his cheeks bulging. "Me too."

"Do you kids like Sunday school and church?" Meemaw asks.

"Ah ... it's okay," Gail says.

"I like the snacks Mrs. Sutcliff gives us every week," Dale adds.

"She likes kids a lot," I say. "Have you learned anything about Jesus in her class?"

"Yeah," Gail says with another mouthful. "He could do miracles. Today we learned that Jesus fed five thousand people with just a small basketful of fish and a few pieces of bread."

"I don't like fish," Dale says, "but I guess if I was there and saw him do that, I'd eat the fish just to eat a miracle!"

Meemaw says, "Kids, Jesus can be your Savior and best friend. He's God, you know. All you need to do is ask him."

I smile as I stare at Meemaw talking about Jesus. She's almost glowing, even though she wears a lot less makeup these days than she used to. I shift my attention to the twins, who have tuned out of the conversation and are digging into their plates like they haven't eaten in a week.

With Captain Ar's words ringing in my ear, I say, "Gail, I saw you played pool really good with Miss McGinnis yesterday. When you earn the privilege to come back to Friday Fun Night at the post, would you like to shoot a game with me?"

Gail looks at me, and her eyes bulge almost big enough to match her bulging cheeks. All she can do is nod like crazy.

"Have you kids ever played Monopoly?" I say.

"What's that?" Dale asks.

"It's a board game that's a lot of fun," I say. "Would you like to play it after we're done eating?"

Gail's mouth is so full, she still can't get a word out. She just nods again with a smile as she chews.

Dale swallows and spurts out, "Yeah. We don't have any games at home. Daddy says we don't have the money for them. I really wanna play it."

At quarter to six on Friday evening, me and Runner are sitting with Captain Ar in her office at her request. She said she wanted an update on our progress with the twins before they would arrive at six for their tutoring hour.

Me and Runner had worked with the kids at their usual time last Monday at the post, and Captain Ar usually talks to us after the twins leave. But last Monday she wasn't there, so Mr. Bill was on duty. When we asked where she was, he said she had an emergency call to the home of one of the new kids and hoped to be back soon. But we never saw her, so she was anxious to hear from us tonight.

"How'd your tutoring time go with the twins on Monday?" Captain Ar, looking sharp in her blue uniform as usual, relaxes in her chair behind a desk stacked with two piles of file folders and papers.

"I guess okay," I say. "Gail still came to me with a face that looked like she was sucking lemons. She asked me three times to help her with a special science assignment. She had to write a report about polar bears. She brought a book about them from the school library, but she had no clue how to start that report. It took almost the whole time, but we got it done."

"How about you, Runner?" Captain Ar asks.

"Well," he says, "Dale came to me twice about his math. He can't get a grasp of mixed fractions and decimals. But the thing that bugged me the most was he kept asking if I had anything to eat. He said he forgot his lunch money and didn't eat anything since breakfast. I felt bad for him, although I wasn't quite sure he was telling the truth. I didn't have any snacks with me, so I told him he'd have to just wait until he got home. After they left, Pockets told me Gail said the same thing to her about lunch. But I guess we'll never know if they were fibbing or not."

"Let's call it what it is," Captain Ar says. "They were lying. I've made sure they have lunch money every day. I stopped in the school weeks ago and gave a check to the principal. I will admit those two have been making some progress since they've started here and are getting to church, but they're masters of deception. It's their defense mechanism to keep them out of trouble, so they think. Just be on guard. Don't fall for their sad little faces if they want something."

"Those little stinkers," I say. "From what Meemaw has told me, they do have it rough at home, but our church ladies are helping out with meals and getting nice clothes for them. They looked really, really nice on Sunday."

Runner slides forward on his chair and raises his finger. "But on Monday, they looked like they hadn't taken a bath in a month, and they had dirty sweatshirts and jeans on. What are they trying to pull?"

"Yeah!" I say. "On Sunday, they had their hair clean, and they were wearing really cute outfits." I pause in deep thought then say, "Oh, but they said their mother helped them get ready. I guess we can pretty much tell when she's sick and in bed by the way they look."

"Kids," Captain Ar says, "remember these two have been deprived for so long, they have certain habits that are hard to break. Now, please understand. I'm not making excuses for them, and I'm praying the counseling they get here will help them be more discerning with what's right and wrong. They haven't yet earned the privilege to come back to Friday Fun Night's activities, and I know that's the thing they really want to do, so we'll use that as a goal for them to achieve."

"At my house last Sunday, I showed them how to play Monopoly," I say. "They went bonkers over it and said they never played any games like that. I wonder if that was a lie."

"I don't think so," Captain Ar says. "I've been to their home several times, and besides not seeing any toys or games during my visits, their mother told me there's never been money to buy the kids much of anything to play with. My heart just aches for them."

DOUBLE TROUBLE AT THE PIONEER TUNNEL

"I think Gail really, really wants to get back to the pool table," I say. "Did you see how good she did with Miss McGinnis?"

"Yes," Captain Ar says. "She's a natural at it."

"I couldn't believe how Gail listened to Miss McGinnis like she did," Runner says. "She doesn't listen to anyone else like that."

"That," Captain Ar says, "might just be the way to gain Gail's trust, Pockets. If you take an interest in her pool game and teach her the basics, you could win a friend forever. It worked here with you when you found out I could shoot. Remember?" She gives me her "got-cha" smile, and my face heats up like I was eating six Fireballs all at one time.

"I sure wish we'd soon see some kind of a change in those two," Runner says. "We're spending an awful lot of time with them, and it doesn't seem to be doing much good."

I mentally count on my fingers the number of times I'll see Gail this week. "Yeah. Counting from last Saturday to this Saturday, I'll be with her five times. We might as well be sisters!"

"What's this Saturday?" Captain Ar asks.

"Oh," I say, "Me and Meemaw are going to the twins' house with some chili. Then we're going to clean up a little around the house."

"Maybe the twins won't even be there," Runner says.

"If you're taking food," Captain Ar says with another smile, "then I think they'll be there."

"You're going to clean the house too?" Runner asks me.

"Well, not really clean it," I say. "Just try to straighten things out a little. From what we've heard, the place is a mess."

"I've never been inside," Runner says. "But I know what the place looks like on the outside just from us picking up the kids for church."

"Just try to be patient," Captain says, leaning forward and folding her hands on the desk. "It's going to take a while, but with all of us showing them love, I think they'll come around. Remember from whence you both came."

"I try to do that all the time when I'm around those two." I glance at Runner, who's just nodding with a subtle smile. I'm pretty sure I know what he's thinking. *Those twins are just impossible.*

Captain Ar glances at the wall clock and stands. "They should be here any minute. You two better get ready for your hour of study. Let's pray we can be kind to them no matter what they do."

"Okay," I say.

"We'll do our best, won't we, Pockets?" Runner gives me that heart-melting wink, and my face heats up again.

"Pockets," she says, "why don't you pray tonight?"

Me? Asked to pray? This woman must be in cahoots with Meemaw. "Oh, all right," I say. "Dear God ..."

CHAPTER THIRTEEN

"Pick us up at eleven o'clock, Tom!" Meemaw tells Pop as she and I—Runner keeps telling me that "she and I" is correct English, not "me and her"—get out of the car in front of the Pawsons' house at nine in the morning.

I don't remember the last time I was in the Heights, the part of Ashland where nobody wants to live. I stare at the Pawsons' two-story house and figure it needed a paint job twenty years ago. The porch is leaning to the left and looks like it's ready to collapse. A couple inches of dirty, caked snow blanket about a half dozen piles of something scattered around in the yard in front of the house. I'm wondering if two of the piles could be the kids' bikes.

I carefully lift a large pot of chili out of the back seat of our car, and Meemaw and I walk to the house as Pop drives away. We balance on a narrow path of flattened, brown snow, since obviously none of the white stuff was ever shoveled off the walkway, if there even is one. As we head up three rickety wooden steps, I notice the porch is stuffed with piles of large, bulging garbage bags and sagging boxes on both sides barely making a way for anyone to get into the house. Although it's so cold we can see our breaths, my nose flinches from a strong, sour smell. Could the bags be full of garbage?

Meemaw knocks on the door, and Gail opens it. "Mommy said you should come in."

DOUBLE TROUBLE AT THE PIONEER TUNNEL

As we tap our boots on the doorstep, I hear someone say, "Ach, don't bother yourselves with the snow on your boots. Come right in."

We step inside the living room, and I have to keep my mouth from dropping open at what I see.

First of all, Gail and Dale, toting rare wide smiles and standing just inches from us, are wearing their best Sunday outfits again, and their hair is neat and clean. But it's only Saturday!

"Hi," the twins say.

"Hello, kids," Meemaw says, and I follow with "Hi."

They look at a woman behind them, and Gail says, "This is our mommy."

On a sunken, dilapidated red and blue checkered sofa sits a very heavy woman with brownish-grey hair drawn back into a ponytail. She's covered from her neck to her knees in a plain tan dress that looks more like a tent. Her eyes look dead tired and sad, and her puffy cheeks are pale—white as milk. Her legs and feet are so swollen, she has no socks or shoes on. She's trying hard to smile through what I think must be a lot of pain. She points behind her shoulder to another adjoining room. I can tell it's the kitchen.

"Honey," she says to me, "just take that pot out there and set it on the table. Thank you both so much for coming and bringing us another meal. I guess you know I'm Hattie, and I believe you are Mona and Tommi Jo?"

For as big as the woman is, I'm surprised at how soft she speaks. Maybe it has something to do with her pain.

"Yes," Meemaw says. "And we're glad to help in any way we can."

As I head to the kitchen, I take a good hard look at the living room, and I see more stacks of sagging boxes in each corner, and I wonder what's in them. I edge my way around two seen-their-better-days dark brown lounge chairs and lopsided end tables with beat-up shiny, red, wood lamps and crooked yellow lampshades that don't match. The dark, wooden floors, scuffed and caked with dirty footprints, have no carpet or throw rugs anywhere. The walls have faded wallpaper with designs of pink roses and green vines. I spot a couple places where the wallpaper has started to peel. I wonder how in a zillion years could we ever clean this place. I remember Meemaw telling me we're the first ones on the schedule. But where do we start?

I hurry into the kitchen and inch the chili on a table already covered with faded blue Melmac dishes caked with left-over food. I glance at the sink and counters that also are heaped with a lot of waiting work. While I head back to the living room, the twins retreat to the sofa, each sitting on either side of their mom, and Dale grabs her hand and caresses it.

"Please have a seat and rest a spell," Hattie says with a painful sigh as she tries to adjust herself in a more comfortable position.

Staring at his mother, Dale squeezes her hand like he'll never let go. She gives him a quick smile then shifts her attention to us.

"We'll sit for just a minute," Meemaw says, "but we came to help clean up a little."

"Oh, you never mind," Hattie says. "Just look at this place. There's not much you can do to make it look presentable. The twins try their best to keep things tidy, but with all these boxes and old furniture ... well ... it's pretty hopeless."

And I try to figure out what they possibly had done to make the place look better.

"You can help us do a big stack of dishes in the kitchen," Gail says.

"Yeah," Dale says. "We kinda got behind on them."

DOUBLE TROUBLE AT THE PIONEER TUNNEL

"We'll be glad to help," Meemaw says. "Won't we, Tommi Jo?"

"Sure," I say, not meaning it at all. I wonder if Captain Ar would say I just lied.

"Hattie," Meemaw says, "have you started your Bible study with Mrs. Sutcliff yet?"

"Yes," she says. "I felt good enough last Wednesday to have her come. It's years since I've been able to get to church. It's so good to hear those old Bible stories again. I can't thank you and your church folks for reaching out to us and getting the twins to Sunday's services."

"We're glad to do it," Meemaw says.

"Lord knows we all need a little religion, don't we?" Hattie brushes a few rebel strands of long hair behind her one ear.

Meemaw slides forward on the chair. "But, Hattie, I'm sure Mrs. Sutcliff has told you that having religion is not what's important. It's our relationship with the Lord Jesus."

"I figure I'm as good as the next guy," Hattie says. "And I've never killed anybody."

"He wants to be your Savior and come into your heart and life," I add.

Meemaw looks at me out of the corner of her eye and subtly shakes her head.

"Mom," Gail says, "can I change my clothes and go out and play now?"

"Yeah," Dale says. "Can we?"

"You can change your clothes, if you'd like," Hattie says. "But you can go outside in a little while. First, I need you to help our guests clean up."

"Okay." They race out of the room, and I hear them storming up a flight of stairs. After a few minutes of Meemaw's chatter with Hattie, the twins come bounding down the stairs. They hurry to their mother's sides again.

Both have on the new sweatshirts and jeans they had worn to snow camp. I guess they had gotten an earful from their mom today to "look nice for the company."

Hattie smiles at us. "Tommi Jo, I also want to thank you and that boy for helping the kids with their schoolwork. I often don't feel well enough to keep after them and check that their homework is done. They've been showing me some of their tests, and their grades are coming up. What's that boy's name who helps Dale?"

"Runner." I give Hattie my best smile. "But that's his nickname. His real name is Vince Ramsey. His parents pick up the kids for church every Sunday."

Hattie's eyes fill with tears. "I can't tell you and the church people how much I appreciate all of this help, especially with these two." She pats the twins' hands. "It's helping to keep them out of trouble."

"We're all glad to do it," Meemaw says again.

"We're ready to help," Dale says. "What should we do?"

"Hattie," Meemaw says, "we'll work on your kitchen. But there's probably not much more we can do but clean up your dishes. Tom will be back for us at eleven. We have to get Tommi Jo some lunch at home before she goes to work at the Sunset Lanes."

"Whatever you can do to help is so much appreciated," Hattie says.

"What'd ya do at the bowling alley?" Gail asks.

"I'm a pinsetter," I say.

"What's that?" Dale asks.

"Me and ... I mean ... Runner and I and two other teens sit behind the pins on different lanes while the bowlers throw the ball at the pins. After the ball knocks over the pins, we crawl down and set up the pins for the bowlers to throw the ball again. Then we have to put the ball on a little track that takes it back to the bowlers too."

"That sounds like a lot of work," Gail says.

"It is, but we get paid," I say.

"We ain't never bowled," Dale says.

"But we'd like to," Gail says.

Hattie sighs. "The money's just not there for them. Doesn't the place have junior leagues on Saturday morning for kids the twins' age?"

"Yep," I say.

"Hey," Meemaw says, "I have an idea."

Uh-oh. I don't like the sound of that.

"Hattie," Meemaw says, "could the kids come home with us today? I'll give them lunch, and we'll get everybody to the bowling alley about twelve thirty. Tommi Jo doesn't start her shift until one. There's always a lunch break there when no one's bowling. She could give them their first lesson. Couldn't you, honey?" She gives me her you're-gonna-do-this smile.

Thanks a lot, Meemaw. Thanks a lot. "Sure, no problem." Another lie?

What is Meemaw thinking?

The twins jump to their feet and their faces light up like the morning sun. "Oh, can we, Mommy?" Gail pleads.

"Sure," Hattie says. "You just help here as much as you can. Then you can go."

"Let's get started!" Dale says. "I can wash the dishes."

"And I'll dry them," Gail says.

"Wait just a minute," Hattie says. "You let Mona run the show out there. She'll tell you what to do."

Meemaw and I stand, and she says to Hattie, "Is there anything we can do for you before we get started?"

"No, I'm fine," she says. "But how much money will the twins need for bowling? If you'll get my purse in the china closet in the kitchen, I'll give you what they need."

"For kids, it's fifty cents a game and ten cents for the shoes," I say. "We'll only have enough time to play one game."

"No, you never mind," Meemaw says to Hattie. "We'll cover the cost of that today."

I'm about ready to blow my stupid mind wondering what in a pig's snout is Meemaw thinking?

Later Saturday, I'm lying on my bed in deep thought after hurrying home at 5:15 from my shift at the lanes. My mind drifts to earlier at the bowling alley.

Runner saved the day concerning the twins! I called him as soon as Meemaw and I got home from the Pawsons' house, and he said he'd come to the lanes early and show Dale how to bowl, while I'd work with Gail.

Although the twins left their stubborn I'll-do-it-my-own-way streak at home, trying to show them how to bowl was still a disaster. They're such pipsqueaks, even a lighter ball didn't help much. The twins kept getting their thumbs caught in the holes, and the ball almost pulled the kids down the lane with them. After a few frames of trying to get them to throw the ball correctly, Runner and I could see that the kids were getting boiling-mad frustrated. So, we ended up just letting them throw the ball with both hands from between their legs. Somehow, they each managed to get a strike once, which Gail said proved that their own way of bowling was just as good as anybody else's. Twerp.

My drifting mind brings me back to now. In a few minutes, I'll go help Meemaw get supper ready. Since we ate our chili at lunch and the twins helped eat every last bean of it, Meemaw decided we'd just have ham salad sandwiches and French fries for supper.

My thoughts wander again to the twins and how ridiculous it was trying to teach them to bowl. I think about their parents, and how it's much easier to understand why

DOUBLE TROUBLE AT THE PIONEER TUNNEL

the kids are the way they are. As Captain Ar said, they're practically raising themselves.

Then I think of my parents, and although Mom and Pop will never live together again, at least I see Pop a lot, and he's been holding down a steady job for months now. That's more than I can say about Parnell. And as far as moms go, at least the twins have one who cares about them even if she can't take care of them. My mom?

I reach to the bottom of the bed and grab my notebook paper and a pen. As usual, I haven't gotten a letter from Mom in quite a while. Although I usually wait to hear from her, I decide to write to her first for a change.

> Dear Mom,
>
> I've been looking for a letter from you the last few days. You must be really busy.
>
> I thought I'd let you know how things are here at home.
>
> Meemaw is feeling much better since her heart attack. She's back to work full-time, and she feels so good, she's helping make meals and doing some cleaning for the Pawson family in town. Hattie, that's the mom, is sick a lot of the time, and Parnell, that's the dad, is ... well ... let's say he has a snoot full lots of times. He doesn't work or help around the house. They have twelve-year-old twins, Gail and Dale. Those two have gotten in a lot of trouble in town, so they're getting counseling from Captain Ar at the Salvation Army post. Captain Ar asked Runner, a friend of mine, and me to help the twins with their studies, and let me tell you, they're a piece of work. They don't want to listen to anybody.

However, since they've started counseling and going to church on Sundays, they're doing a little better. That's exactly what happened to me. I guess you remember how messed up I was, but then Captain Ar told me about Jesus, and when I asked him to be my Savior, everything changed in my life. Meemaw did that too, and she's been happier than she's ever been.

I know you don't care to hear anything about Pop, but he's doing a little better. He's holding down a job at Teichmans' Garage downtown. And guess what else changed with him? He's not going to bars anymore. He bought a couple cases of booze and is helping himself to the bottles at home. We're real glad he's staying home more now because the only time he comes in real late is when he's shooting pool at Joe's, but that's usually only on Saturday nights.

I'm doing pretty good in school. On my last report card, I got an A in science! I got B's in everything else except algebra. I got a C in that again. I'd probably be flunking it if Runner wasn't helping me. He and I are still working at the Sunset Lanes downtown. We put in ten hours a week. That extra money really helps Meemaw's budget. It almost pays for all the groceries for the week.

Well, I just wanted to write and say hello and that I love you. Mom, I pray for you every day that you'll believe in Jesus as your Savior. You'll never be happier. I hope you start going to church too. Please write to me soon and let me know how you're doing. Are

DOUBLE TROUBLE AT THE PIONEER TUNNEL

you still planning to come east this summer?
I hope so. I miss you.

    Your daughter,
    Tommi Jo

I fold the letter then think about the letter I gave Pop a while back. He never said a word about it. I wonder what happened to it. Then I think I should write him another letter, maybe just a short note. I grab another piece of paper and start.

Dear Pop,

    I just wanted to write a note to thank you for being my dad. I'm glad you're able to work more these days, and Meemaw and I are really, really glad you're not going to bars anymore.

    Pop, I just want to say I love you, and we're praying that you will soon take Jesus into your life. You'll be so much happier than you are now. And I want you to be with Meemaw and me in heaven someday. I love you.

    Your daughter,
    Tommi Jo

I fold that paper, hop off the bed, stuff the letters in two envelopes, and head downstairs to help Meemaw. I think I'll put Pop's letter in his lunch bucket. He can't miss it there!

CHAPTER FOURTEEN

Gail whacks the cue ball, knocks the orange five ball in a corner pocket, and smiles like she just won a million bucks. "Yes!" she says raising her pool stick in the air.

"That's good, Gail," I say. "Real good."

It's Friday night in mid-March, and "Captain Ar's kids" are at the post. The weather has warmed up a bit, the snow has melted, and we've put our heavy coats and winter boots away. I saw two flocks of geese heading north last week. I'm really hoping we don't get any more snow. Even though I'm still a kid, I'm tired of the flakes and want to see more sun and green grass. I know my bike is just itching to get out of that shed in the backyard.

Over the last few weeks, the twins have been keeping their noses clean as well as their clothes, so Captain Ar gave them permission to come to Fun Night again. Of course, Runner and I are working with them on their pool game. Gail's picking it up like a little trooper, but her brother just doesn't have what it takes.

"Aw rats." Dale grits his teeth as he watches the cue ball go in a side pocket after his miscue. "I can't get this," he growls. "Let's do something else."

I can tell he's really starting to boil inside because his freckles even turn red when he gets so hot under the collar.

"All right, Dale." Runner points to an empty card table along the left wall. "How about some Checkers?"

DOUBLE TROUBLE AT THE PIONEER TUNNEL

"Anything's better than pool," Dale grumbles and mounts his stick on the wall rack.

While Runner and Dale head to the card table, I glance around the room and watch all my friends having a ball. Coochie and Reuben are playing ping-pong, Moose and Mr. Bill are playing darts, and Captain Ar, Trudy, and Leona are at one of the corner tables playing a card game. The kitchenette counter is loaded with a big plate of sandwiches, chips, cupcakes, and bottles of Coke.

The two new boys, Boomer and Nick, aren't here. Runner told me Boomer smart-mouthed the school principal and got detention, and Nick lost his temper after getting an F on a history test and slammed his locker door so hard, he bent it. So, they're both on probation again. Idiots. They probably won't get invited back here until Christmas!

I take my turn shooting and run four balls off in a row, cleaning off the table. Just as I knock off the last ball, Leona and Trudy join us. I glance at Captain Ar and she's doing something at the food counter while her attention is focused our way.

"Hey, Pockets," Leona says, sweeping her long wavy hair back off her brow, "can we shoot?"

"Yeah." Trudy's chubby cheeks court her dimpled smile. "Captain Ar beat us bad at Crazy Eights. We thought maybe we can do better at pool."

"Sure, you—"

"I'm shootin' with Pockets," Gail barks. "Just wait your turn."

"I thought you two just finished your umpteenth game," Leona says. "C'mon. It's our turn."

Gail's face turns as red as the three ball. "I'm not done yet!"

I take a quick look at Captain Ar who's watching us like a hawk zeroing in on a brood of squabbling chickens. If I know Captain Ar, I think this is a set-up to see how Gail will react. How any of us will react. How I will react.

This time I think real hard before I open my big, fat mouth. A verse Captain Ar had me memorize pops up in my mind like a firecracker going off. The book of Proverbs, chapter fifteen, verse one says, "A soft answer turneth away wrath: but grievous words stir up anger." I figure I can either calm the kid down or watch her explode. It all depends on how I talk to her.

Like I'm on eggshells, I walk next to Gail and give her my best smile. "Aw, c'mon, Gail. I know you like board games. I've been wanting to teach you how to play Parcheesi. I bet you'll be real good at it. We can shoot some more after snack time. What'd ya say?"

"Yeah," Leona says. "We'll only play a game or two."

"Please with whipped cream on top ..." Trudy adds.

Gail stands with her arms crossed and her feet planted firm on the floor. She stares at me with a hateful scowl and looks like she's ready to let it rip. She glances at the other girls, then shifts her attention to Captain Ar, who's staring back.

Silence invades the entire room as Mr. Bill and the boys zoom in and brace themselves for a volcanic eruption.

"Oh, all right," Gail says. "I'm tired of shooting anyway." She puts her stick on the rack and walks to the card table without another word.

With a sigh of relief, I glance at Captain Ar and smile.

She smiles all the way to her blue eyes and gives me a thumbs up.

I feel like we all just got A's in a Kid Maturity test at Post 71.

And this time I remember to thank God. He made it all happen.

DOUBLE TROUBLE AT THE PIONEER TUNNEL

Sunday morning, Meemaw and I had to walk the six blocks to church. The weather is not too cold for mid-March, and the snow has all melted, so we didn't need our heavy coats or boots to slow us down.

Pop didn't drive us there because he never came home last night, which is worrying me to the high hilt. It's been weeks since he's pulled that stunt, and I'm wondering if he went back to his favorite hangout and got in some kind of trouble. Maybe he and Parnell got into a fight, and Pop could be conked out in a ditch somewhere. I'm praying like crazy that's not the case.

After church, Pop never came to pick us up either, so Meemaw and I are walking home. We've only got a block to go. I know something's wrong with Pop. I just know it.

"Meemaw," I say as we trudge up Market Street, "what do you think happened to Pop?"

"I don't know," Tommi Jo," she says. "I'm a little concerned about him."

"You know it's been weeks since he's stayed out all night long."

"Yes, I know. Maybe he'll be home when we get there."

"I sure hope so." Then I change the subject. "Right after church, I saw Runner for a few minutes. He said his dad would have offered to take us home, but their car was already full. Today they were taking Gail and Dale home for the afternoon."

"The Ramseys are very kind folks, aren't they?" Meemaw says.

"Yes, and Runner said his mom even made a turkey dinner for the twins, and he planned to teach them how to play Monopoly. When I reminded him I'd already taught them that game at our place, he said he'd show them how to play Clue. These twins are being treated like movie stars."

"Aw, Tommi Jo, not really. It's the first time in their lives that anyone's probably paid any attention to them.

Didn't they look cute this morning? Gail had on her light blue sweater and that cute, navy blue poodle skirt. And Dale had his light blue sweater on with navy blue pants. I know Mrs. Sutcliff bought them those outfits, and the twins looked adorable."

"I noticed their hair was neat and clean too, so their mom must have felt good enough to help them get ready for church. I wonder if their dad is *ever* home."

"Now that I'm getting to know Hattie a little better, she's opening up to me. She told me that sometimes it's better if Parnell isn't home, especially when he's been drinking a lot. He's hit the kids more than once, and hard, for no reason."

"Why doesn't she call the cops?"

"That's a hard question to answer. She might feel that she has to put up with him as long as he, somehow, manages to pay the bills. She told me the money they get from the government is always sent in his name. If he'd leave or have to go to jail, she doesn't know what she'd do."

"I guess that's why she's so thankful our church is helping."

"Yes. But she also told me if he keeps hitting the kids, she'll have no choice but to report him. And with the Sutcliffs and our church folks helping out, we're all praying the whole family comes to the Lord. Wouldn't that be wonderful?"

"You bet," I say as we reach our house.

After walking six blocks, Meemaw is huffing pretty bad.

"Are you okay, Meemaw?" I ask as we get to our front door.

"Sure," she huffs. "I'm just a little winded. We haven't done that hike in quite a while. I guess I'm out of shape."

I turn and look at her. "Are you sure you're okay?"

DOUBLE TROUBLE AT THE PIONEER TUNNEL

"Yes, Tommi Jo. I'm all right. Now stop worrying."

We step inside, and I hear a noise coming from the kitchen, like running water. "Listen, Meemaw. I hear something."

"I'm sure it's not a giant mouse helping himself to our dinner," she says with a chuckle. "I think your father might be home."

We hurry to the kitchen, and Pop's standing at the sink with a bottle of beer. Three boxes of booze are sitting on the table.

Pop turns to us, his face draped in surprise. "Wha-what are you girls doing home so early?"

"It's not early, Pop," I say. "It's quarter after twelve."

He glances at the wall clock. "Hm-m-m, I guess it is."

"What are you up to, Tom?" Meemaw says.

Pop sets his bottle on the counter next to four more bottles that look empty. He sighs. "I need to talk to you both. Come sit down." He takes the boxes off the table and sets them on the floor.

"Can't this wait until after we eat dinner?" Meemaw asks.

"No, I want to talk to you both right now. I've waited long enough."

Meemaw and I take our coats off and throw them over the back of one of the chairs. Pop and I sit while Meemaw goes to her slow cooker. She takes a peek inside, puts the lid back on, and turns off the cooker. "The ham and potatoes are in good shape. They can wait." She comes and sits at the table. "What is it, Tom? And where were you last night? We were awful worried about you."

"Yeah," I say. "What's wrong? Are you sick or something?"

"No, I'm not sick." Pop leans forward on his folded hands. They're shaking a little. "And I did come home about one o'clock."

"I didn't hear you," I say.

"I didn't either," Meemaw says.

"That's because I snuck in, but I didn't go to bed. I spent the rest of the night sitting in the basement, staring at all these boxes." He points to the stack next to him.

Meemaw and I just sit and stare at him.

"Tommi Jo ..." Pop says, and his eyes water like he's starting to cry.

I have never ever seen him cry. I know he's not plastered. If he was, I'd smell the beer on his breath. *So, what's happening here?*

"Pop, what's the matter?" Now my eyes start floating. "Are you dying?"

"Thomas Leland, tell us," Meemaw orders. "Right this minute!"

"Mona," Pop says, "I want you to call Pastor Sutcliff. I need to talk to him."

"Why, Pop, why?" I ask.

"Girls," he says, "I've watched you the last year or so since you got religion. I've watched you very carefully. Tommi Jo, I've never seen such a change in anyone. And, Mona, with everything you've been through with your heart attack and all, you still praise your God and have a smile on your face. Both of you have changed so much. You don't just think of yourselves anymore either. You're so willing to help others."

"That's because we took Jesus into our hearts, Pop," I say.

"It's God who changed us," Meemaw says.

"I know, I know," he says and looks at me with tears trickling down his cheeks. "And the final straw was your letters. Nobody has ever told me they loved me ... until you came along."

"The letters?" I ask. "Pop, you've never said anything about my letters."

DOUBLE TROUBLE AT THE PIONEER TUNNEL

Pop pulls my letters out of his shirt pocket and lays them on the table. "I've read these over and over and over. I'm beginning to realize what real love is." He looks at Meemaw and then me. "When you told me you love me, and I read all those verses you wrote that tell about God and how much he loves us, the truth started to sink into my hard heart."

"Tom," Meemaw says, "we've been praying for you every day."

"You both seem so happy," he says. "You have something I don't have, and I want it. I need to talk to Pastor Sutcliff."

"Why don't you go to church with us next week?" Meemaw says.

"I can't wait that long. I want to see him today," Pop says.

"I'll call him right now!" I say.

Pop wipes his eyes on his sleeve. "Okay."

I rush to the phone in the living room. I look up his number in the phone book and dial. In seconds, a man answers the phone.

"Hello, Pastor Sutcliff," I say, wiping my eyes on my sleeve, "can you come to our house right away?"

CHAPTER FIFTEEN

It's Monday afternoon, and Runner and I are having our study hour with the twins at the post. Earlier, Captain Ar had a session with Runner and me before the kids got here. I couldn't wait to tell her what happened yesterday.

I've been floating on Cloud Nine.

Sunday afternoon, Pastor Sutcliff came to our house and talked to Pop for three hours. Pop asked Jesus into his heart and life. As soon as Pastor Sutcliff left, Pop took every last one of his bottles of booze and dumped them down the drain. He said he never, ever wanted to touch the stuff again. And he said he wanted to go to church with us next Sunday. I think he really means it, and I might have myself a brand new daddy.

Now, as Runner and I help the twins with their homework, it's hard to concentrate on what I'm doing. But, as usual, Captain Ar has come to my rescue. I keep thinking of what she just told Runner and me a few minutes ago, and I can't get her words out of my mind.

"Pockets, do you know what brought your father to the Lord?"

I think for a few seconds then say, "Well, we've been praying like crazy for him. And Pop said it's the way Meemaw and I have changed."

"Well, that's part of it. But the key is love. You both reached out to him with a special love that God gave you for him even though he didn't deserve it. None of us really deserve God's love."

Runner smiles. "And I remember you telling us it's all because of God's grace."

I nod and smile too.

"Now, I want you to try really hard to do something today with the twins," Captain Ar says as she opens her Bible. "Listen to this verse. 'And above all things have fervent charity among yourselves: for charity shall cover the multitude of sins.' That verse is in First Peter chapter four, verse eight. Kids, the word charity there means love. It's an action word."

"Okay," I say. "What would you like us to do?"

She leans forward. "I'd like you to tell the twins you love them. Of course, Runner you tell Dale, and Pockets, you tell Gail."

"You've got to be kidding," I say. "How can we do that when we *don't* love them?"

"Ah, here's the difference." Captain Ar closes her Bible and points at us. "God can and will give you a special love for them ... if you're willing. Do you know you can have God's love for those two even though you don't like them? As you let God love those kids through you, you eventually will start to like them."

"Hm-m-m," Runner says. "I never thought of that before."

"Me neither," I say.

"I'm sure you'd like to see those twins happy and staying out of trouble, wouldn't you?"

"You said it." Runner sighs. "But they're so stinkin' stubborn."

"How many people do you think ever told the twins they loved them?"

"Zero," I say.

"Maybe their mom," Runner adds.

"Don't you think it would mean so much to those kids if you two would tell them you love them? Remember, it's God who will give you that love. Oh, yes, you've been showing them a little love by helping them. But is it really from your hearts or just because I asked you to do it?"

We just stare at her.

"If you really want to see a change in those two, then there has to be a change in you two," she says. "And remember this. Love covers a multitude of sins."

While Captain Ar's words rattle my brain, Gail's sitting next to me waiting for me to help her with her spelling homework. How she and her brother can turn from Doctor Jekyll into Mr. Hyde in one measly day is beyond me. Gail's sour face matches her messed-up, straggly pigtails and her wrinkled, dirty clothes. They both look like the ragamuffins we knew when we first met them. I guess their mother has taken to bed again.

"Gail," I say, smiling, "let's do a review of your twenty words. Then I'll give you a test on all of them. Okay?"

"Okay." She pushes her spelling book across the card table to me and just slumps in her chair, staring down. She looks so pitiful, for the first time in my selfish life, I actually feel sorry for the kid. "Love covers a multitude of sins," echoes in my head.

"Gail, what's the matter?" I ask.

"Nothin'." She never looks at me.

"Gail ..."

I wait ... and wait ... until she looks at me.

"I love you, Gail," I say, "and I really do want to help you."

For the first time ever, our eyes lock, her bottom lip starts to quiver, and tears flood her eyes. "I—I—"

I open her spelling book and smile at her. "C'mon. Let's get these spelling words learned."

DOUBLE TROUBLE AT THE PIONEER TUNNEL

It's a week later on Monday afternoon, and Runner and I are in Captain Ar's office waiting for her. She's doing something in the game room. Mr. Bill, as usual, is picking up the twins at school.

In a few minutes, Captain Ar comes in, sits behind her desk, and opens two files. "So, how about an update on the twins. Did either of you manage to do what I asked since last Monday? And if so, have you noticed if their behavior around you has changed at all?"

Runner starts. "I told Dale I loved him last Monday in our study hour. He said, 'Aw rats,' then told me I was full of baloney and that I should go adopt a puppy. I haven't seen any change in him except, maybe, he doesn't sit anymore with his arms crossed and a face mad enough to scare the boogeyman."

Captain Ar and I burst out laughing, and Runner joins in. I can't help but stare holes through him today. He's wearing his fire engine red pullover shirt with a white collar and black trousers. Add his wavy, dark hair and chocolate-brown eyes, and he's one dreamy hunk. When he smiles at me, I feel like my heart's going to take off after him and leave me behind.

"Pockets," Captain Ar says, "how about you and Gail?"

"Well, I told Gail I loved her last Monday too, and she almost started bawling right in front of me. She was speechless. When we did all her homework, she didn't seem to be so obnoxious. She actually listened to me. Then on Friday night when we were shooting pool, she didn't argue when some of the other kids wanted their turn."

"Yes," Captain Ar says. "I noticed that too. This is all a good sign with her."

"I just wish our telling them we love them would motivate them to take baths and wear clean clothes," Runner says.

"Now don't forget what's going on at their home," Captain Ar says. "They probably have no idea how to wash their clothes."

"And forget ironing," I add. "But I heard Meemaw talking on the phone with somebody, and they were figuring out how to help in that area too."

"That's wonderful." Captain Ar glances at the wall clock. "I wonder where Bill and the kids are. They're fifteen minutes late.

Just then, Mr. Bill comes hurrying in from outside, his hair bristled from the March wind and his chubby cheeks flushed. "The kids weren't at pick-up," he huffed. "When I checked with Principal Dimock, he said they left school without permission early this morning. Then he explained why. He just happened to be in the hallway when the first-hour classes dismissed. At the same time, Sergeant Bailey came in the school and asked to see the twins. The men headed toward the kids' homeroom and spotted them at their lockers. When the kids saw Sergeant Bailey, they grabbed their jackets and took off like two jack rabbits. The men ran after the twins but couldn't catch them.

"Sergeant Bailey asked to look in the kids' lockers where he found two small paper bags overflowing with candy. The sergeant told the principal that before school this morning, two kids went behind the counter at Tony Kievel's corner store when Tony had gone into his back room for something, and they took hands full of candy, stuffing the candy in two paper bags. Before Tony could catch them, they took off."

"Oh, brother," I say. "And we thought we were making progress with those twins."

Mr. Bill continues. "Tony reported it to the police. He didn't know the two kids, a girl and a boy, but from his description, Sergeant Bailey knew it was the Pawson twins because of their past record. I asked Mr. Dimock why he didn't call us, and he said he called the kids' home and their father answered, but he didn't seem too concerned. The principal made a point to tell Mr. Pawson to be sure to call us."

"He never did," Captain Ar says.

"Should I go to the Pawsons' home and see if they're there?" Mr. Bill asks.

Captain Ar pushes away from her desk and stands. "No, Bill. You stay here and hold down the fort. We'll go." She points to Runner and me. "I'd like you to come with me. You might be able to help when I confront them." She picks up her phone receiver and hands it to me. "Both of you please call your parents and tell them what happened and what we're doing just so they know you're all right if you don't get home at the usual time."

Ten minutes later, we pull in front of the Pawsons' house. A police car with flashing lights is already stationed there.

The three of us rush up on the porch, knock, and hear a man say, "Come in."

We hurry in but stop right inside the doorway.

Sergeant Bailey is sitting on the sofa next to Hattie, who's bawling her eyes out.

I don't doubt for one minute Sergeant Bailey made her cry. I've had more than one run-in with that guy. I used to call him "Sergeant Know-It-All" because I thought he was so cocky. He's a huge beast of a man in a bright blue uniform, his brown hair in a crewcut and his wide, black leather belt armed with a pistol, handcuffs, a billy club, and keys. I found out pretty quick not to mess with this cop. But Meemaw told me I need to have respect for the law, and now I try real hard to do that. He can't help it if he scares little kids and makes mothers cry. It's just part of his job, I guess.

"Ah, Captain Masters!" Sergeant Bailey says. "I see you have two of your kids with you. Tommi Jo and Vince, I do believe. I suppose you're here for the same reason I am."

"Yes," Captain Ar says. "We're very concerned about the twins. Are they here?"

Hattie struggles to speak through her sobbing. "They never came home today after they ran away from school. I had no idea what they had done. I know they left here scared out of their wits this morning. Their father was on one of his rampages and threatened to beat the tar out of them."

"Where's Parnell?" the sergeant asks Hattie, his face looking like he really is concerned.

"I don't know." Hattie dabs her eyes with an already-soaked hanky. "He's hardly ever here."

Captain Ar hurries to the woman, sits next to her, and touches her shoulder gently. "Hattie, we need to find the twins. Where do you think they are?"

"I have no idea," she says. "I know they've gotten into a lot of trouble. Lord knows I've tried my best to raise those two, but I haven't been able to do much with my ailment."

"We know that," Captain Ar says.

"Now think," the policeman says to Hattie. "Where could they have gone? We need to find them, not because of what they did, but they've been missing too long. My men and I have canvassed the whole town, up and down every street, every park, several times. We might soon have to put out an APB for them."

"Sergeant," Captain Ar says, "don't you usually have to wait twenty-four hours for an All-Points Bulletin?"

"In this case with kids so young, I feel we can't wait that long. Children wandering where they shouldn't wander can put themselves in a lot of danger."

DOUBLE TROUBLE AT THE PIONEER TUNNEL

I lean close to Runner and whisper, "I think I know where they are."

"Where?" he whispers back.

"The Pioneer Tunnel. Remember when we confronted them in the park a while back? They knew where that old mine shaft was."

"That's right!" Runner glances at the three on the sofa then whispers to me, "You better say something."

"Captain Ar," I say.

"Yes, Pockets."

"We think we know where the twins are."

Sergeant Bailey stands and faces us. "Where? We've got to find those kids."

"They might be hiding in the deserted Pioneer Tunnel in the hill behind the Higher Ups Park," Runner says.

"Yes," the man says. "I know all about that mine. But I didn't think to have my men check that out."

"Yeah," I say. "A while back when we were at the park, the twins showed up, and to make a long story short, they saw us and hightailed it to the mine. We followed them and stopped them before they could squeeze through the boards blocking the entrance. But those two are small enough to easily get through and hide in there."

"Oh, no!" Hattie's tears start flowing again. "They could get lost in there. I remember reading in the newspaper a few months ago that there are different tunnels that branch out for hundreds of yards inside the hill. Oh, please go look for them. Please."

Sergeant Bailey says, "We will. I'll head there right now."

Captain Ar stands and gives Hattie another reassuring pat on the woman's shoulder. "Don't you worry. We'll find them." She joins us and says, "Sergeant, we're going to drive there too. We'll see if there are any signs that the kids are in the mine."

"All right," he says. "It might be a good idea if they know you're outside. If they just hear or see me, they might go back farther into the mine."

"Right," Captain Ar says. "We'll see you there."

"Gail! Dale! Can you hear me!" Captain Ar yells into the mine shaft, the opening still blocked by a frame of four wide boards. One board had been pried off and lies on the ground. "It's me, Captain Ar. Kids, if you're in there, please come out. Pockets and Runner are here too. We're here to help you. Please!"

"Gail!" I yell, my words echoing far into the tunnel. "Are you in there?"

"Dale!" Runner yells. "It's me, Runner. Come on out! Nobody's gonna hurt you!"

I hear a car pulling in at the park border. In a short minute, Sergeant Bailey hurries out from the thicket and joins us. "Are they in there?" he asks.

"We're not sure," Captain Ar says. "But if they are in there and they know you're here, they might never come out."

"All right," he says. "You just try to connect with them. I'll stay in the background."

Captain Ar nods at him, then turns back to the mine entrance. "Kids, are you in there?"

"Just go away!" Dale's voice echoes. "We're not ever coming out."

"Gail!" I yell. "It's me, Pockets. Please come out."

"No!" Gail yells.

"I'll go in and get them." I grip one of the boards and try to pry it loose.

Captain Ar grabs my arm and pulls me away. "Oh, no you don't. It's too dangerous."

DOUBLE TROUBLE AT THE PIONEER TUNNEL

"Somebody's got to go in," Runner says. "Let me."

"No," Sergeant Bailey says. "If they soon don't come out, I'll call the fire department."

I press against the boards and yell, "Gail, please come out!"

"No," Gail yells. "We don't want to go to jail!"

Captain Ar yells, "Gail, we know about the candy. But you won't go to jail. You'll just spend more time with me at the post. Please come out! Your mother is so worried about you!"

"No!" Dale's voice echoes. "We won't—"

A terrifying noise that sounds like thunder rumbles above us, and the ground starts shaking. A small haze of dust slams into our faces, and I fling my arm over my face.

"Everyone, get back!" Sergeant Bailey shouts, wiping his eyes with his sleeve. "It sounds like a cave-in!"

Coughing, we back far away from the mouth of the mine as the rumbles get louder and then—

Crash!

The loudest sound I've ever heard explodes as a flood of boulders and rocks fills the opening of the mine. An enormous cloud of dust zooms out from the mine and envelops us.

The noise, the dust, the shaking all end as quickly as it started.

Coughing, I stand and stare at the mine, now sealed with a wall of debris. "No!" I scream. "They're still in there!"

As the dust settles, we wipe off our faces and rush to the mine. We have to throw some bowling ball-sized boulders aside just to get to where the KEEP AWAY boards used to be. Now the opening is not open anymore, stacked to the top with all sizes of rocks and grit that will take picks and shovels to get through.

"Gail!" Captain Ar screams. "Dale, can you hear me?"

No answer.

"What'll we do?" I start bawling and look at three faces draped in pure panic.

Runner starts throwing rocks to the side. "We have to start digging!"

Sergeant Bailey runs toward the thicket. "I'll call the fire department and get my men to help dig. They'll be here in a few minutes with equipment to open up that hole." In seconds he's gone.

"Gail!" I yell, then I join Captain Ar and Runner in removing debris from the opening.

Still no answer.

About fifty rocks and fifteen minutes later, I hear fire engine horns and police car sirens coming closer ... closer ... closer.

A few minutes later, a small army of policemen, ambulance crew, and firemen in their helmets, tan suits, and equipment arrive.

"Stand back!" A man with a fire chief helmet points at us.

We do as he says, and he and nine other men attack the debris.

I notice that Sergeant Bailey hasn't come back. I'm wondering if he went to tell the twins' mother what has happened.

Captain Ar, Runner, and I stand to the side, our eyes flooding with tears as the men pick at the rock pile and shovel away debris.

"Kids," Captain Ar says to us, "if there was ever a time to pray, it's now."

"Faster, men!" the fire chief yells. "If the kids are still okay, there might be very little air for them to breathe."

The men work at the debris and pull boulders away as fast as they can.

Finally, they break through, making an opening at eye level about the size of a basketball.

DOUBLE TROUBLE AT THE PIONEER TUNNEL

"We're through!" one of the firemen yells. "Kids," he yells into the hole, "can you hear me! Kids!"

No answer.

The fireman pushes away handfuls of debris and stretches to see through the hole. "I think I can see them through the settling dust. Kids, can you hear me?"

"C'mon," Captain Ar says to us, and we hurry to join the men.

"Sir!" She grabs the chief's arm. "I'm Captain Masters from the Salvation Army. Those kids in there are in my counseling program. Their parents aren't here." She points to Runner and me. "These two are good friends of the twins. Please let us see if they'll answer us."

"Just for a minute," he says. "We've got to clear away more debris to get in there. And quick!"

We follow Captain Ar as she rushes toward the opening.

I grab her arm. "Please, Captain Ar, let me see if they'll answer me. Please."

"Okay, Pockets, go ahead. Oh, dear God, I pray they're all right."

"Men," the fire chief says, "back away and stop just for a minute. Everybody, quiet!"

The men stop and stand in silence. Waiting.

I stick my head almost through the basketball-sized hole. "Gail! It's me, Pockets! Can you hear me!"

"Y-yes!" Gail says and coughs.

"Are you all right?" I yell through the hole.

"W-we're okay," Dale says with a cough. "But ... it's ... it's hard to breathe."

Runner steps next to me. "Dale! It's me, Runner. We'll get you out in a minute."

"Just back away from the pile," Captain Ar yells to the twins. "There are men here to help get you out!"

"Okay," they yell.

Captain Ar, Runner, and I back away, and the men start digging again. In minutes they have enough of an opening for the twins to crawl out. As they do, two firemen lift them and carry them away from the mine. The kids are covered from head to toe in a grey dust, but they look okay. I don't see even a scratch on either one.

Everyone releases an echoing cheer, and as the firemen steady the kids on their feet, we rush to the twins' sides.

"Are you both really all right?" The chief crouches in front of the twins.

"We're okay, I think," Dale says. "We moved far back just like you said."

"We'll have our ambulance team check you out." The chief turns to one of his men. "Hank, get your equipment."

"Yes, sir," Hank replies.

"You other men," the chief orders, "start closing the mouth. We need to shut this mine so that no one can ever get inside again." He joins his men as they start to shovel.

Gail turns, runs toward me, and wraps her arms around my waist. She's shaking like she's been swimming in ice-cold water.

Dale runs into Runner's open arms. "We're sorry we took the candy," Dale says.

"We know you are," Runner says and gives him a hug. Through teary eyes, he adds, "Love ya, buddy!"

I bend down and hold Gail at shoulder's length. Eyes still moist, I say, "Gail, I'm so glad you're not hurt. Remember, I love you." I draw her into a soft embrace.

As Gail looks up, her eyes flood with tears that make tracks down her dirty cheeks.

Captain Ar joins our huddle. She kneels so she's at eye level with the twins. "I am so glad you are all right."

"You're crying!" Gail says and rushes into her waiting arms.

"Yeah," Dale says as he looks at the three of us. "You're crying. You're all crying."

"It's because we love you," Captain Ar says. "And we mean it."

DOUBLE TROUBLE AT THE PIONEER TUNNEL

Gail backs away from Captain Ar, looks at me, and gives me a smile I didn't think she had. "And I-I love you."

"Aw rats," Dale says with a smile that bursts through his dirty face. "I love you guys, and I mean it too."

The End

THE AUTHOR AND HER OWN POP

Where did the author, Marsha Hubler, get the idea to write about Pockets and her pop?

Marsha grew up in a home where her own pop was not a Christian, but her mother was.

Marsha and her mother prayed for many years for Marsha's pop to give his heart and life to the Lord Jesus Christ. When Marsha grew up, got married, and left her parents' home, she wrote letters to her father just like Pockets wrote to her pop in the story.

When Marsha's pop finally became a Christian, he did two things just like Pockets' father did in the story. One, he gave back all the letters Marsha had written to him over many years and told her he had read them many times. He never threw away one of her letters. Two, he

DOUBLE TROUBLE AT THE PIONEER TUNNEL

carried up two cases of beer and wine from his basement and poured every bottle down the drain and never drank alcohol again.

Marsha's pop had a new way of living with his faith in Jesus. He went to heaven in 1998 at the age of 85.

ABOUT THE AUTHOR

Marsha Hubler is the author of the best-selling Keystone Stables Series and fourteen other books. She has a master's degree in special needs and is a homeschool consultant, an educator of children of all ages for over forty-eight years, and the director of the Montrose Christian Writers Conference. She grew up in Ashland, Pennsylvania, where her father taught her to shoot pool when she was tall enough to reach the table. She still enjoys a game now and then with her dad's pool table in her game room. Visit her at www. marshahublerauthor.com.

IS THE PIONEER TUNNEL A REAL PLACE?

Although this book about Captain Ar and "her kids" from Ashland, Pennsylvania, is fiction, there really is a tourist attraction in Ashland, Pennsylvania, called "The Pioneer Tunnel and Steam Lokie."

Ashland lies in coal country in eastern Pennsylvania. In its heyday during the 1930s and 40s, the coal business in the state boomed. But in the 1950s, the coal mines shut down, leaving many mines abandoned like the Pioneer Tunnel. Some mines flooded with water. Others just grew shut with rockslides and dense foliage. That's what happened to the Pioneer Tunnel. But in 1961, some folks in town, members of the Ashland Community Enterprises, got a brilliant idea.

"Let's make it into a tourist attraction," one man said.

"And the Higher Ups Park is right next to the mine for families to have a picnic and relax," another man said.

"We need a lot of money," another man said. "But I think we can do this!"

So, with donations of thousands of dollars and a very large government loan, the project began in 1961. By 1962, the mine opened to visitors and the little train engine, nicknamed "the Lokie," became part of the attraction.

At first, visitors could only walk inside the mine while the Lokie pulled a few cars, taking guests on a ride around the mountain. Eventually, after men removed tons and tons of rocks from inside the mine, battery-operated cars started taking guests 1800 feet inside the Mahanoy Mountain to explore an underground coal mine.

As of today, the tourist attraction has had hundreds of thousands of visitors, over 40,000 every year. Where a deep hole in the ground once lay dormant, now Ashland is proud to have a tourist attraction complete with a souvenir gift shop and snack bar. And the Higher Ups Park is still there for visitors to enjoy as well.

The Pioneer Tunnel and Steam Lokie attraction is open from April to October. Learn more about it at Pioneer Tunnel and Pioneer Tunnel Ashland.

www.ingramcontent.com/pod-product-compliance
Ingram Content Group UK Ltd.
Pitfield, Milton Keynes, MK11 3LW, UK
UKHW021311180426
11947UKWH00015B/1154